哈福

哈福

輕鬆打開

「英語」

Daily English 話匣子

大家的第一本英語

附 MP3

蘇盈盈・Lily Thomas ◎合著

哈福

輕鬆打開
英語話匣子

在電梯裡，聽到「哈囉」聲時，你是熱情地和他們打招呼，或是冷眼以對？

拿起電話，聽到「哈囉」聲時，你會怎麼處理？是心跳加快，不知所云，只想趕快把電話掛掉，或是到處找救兵呢？

如果你是屬於後面的這類族群，就是該奮發圖強，熟讀本書的時候了。

本書收錄的內容，都是生活上，你可能碰到的對話，非常實用，非常簡單，簡直用直覺就可以學會，是您成為英語高手的跳板。

不論是跟朋友互動或是交際應酬，出外購物與店員的交談，甚至是看醫生、買藥等生活上大大小小的瑣事，本書都蒐羅相當齊全。

本書內容皆為日常生活中的生活對話，不管面臨結交外國朋友，或是出國旅行都相當實用，讓你不再是英語啞巴！為了克服你學習語言的障礙，建議你從生活中的口語開始！絕對能夠讓你 Fun 輕鬆説英語。

　　超實用生活會話，搭配專業標準發音 MP3，相信你的舌頭不會再打結，你的腦袋沒有時間空白，你的嘴巴沒有機會停下來。如果你想秀一口流利的英語，那麼，本書絕對可以幫你達成心願。

　　「情境對話」是生活中常會用到的談話內容；「句型解析」則讓讀者一次學到多種不同的説法；「單字片語」包括音標、單字的淵源及註解；「小錦囊」是作者搜集的一些生活小常識，供讀者參考；「課後小點心」有風俗民情及小故事，休息一下，再繼續衝刺，效果加倍！

　　千萬不要小看生活上的小細節，和老外聊天時，怎麼表達最貼切，這是門很大的學問，多加磨練，是絕對必要的。

　　學英語，就從你的生活中開始吧！把握每個可以練習的機會，説英語就自然變得很簡單了。

編者　謹識

前言
輕鬆打開英語話匣子

Part 1 英語會話第一步

Chapter 1 邀請篇 Inviting

Chapter 2 購物篇 Shopping

Chapter 8 打電話篇 Telephoning

Part 2 英語會話第二步

Chapter 1 度假、休假 Vacation

Chapter 2 社交活動 SOCIAL ACTIVITY

Chapter 3 嗜好和運動 HOBBY/SPORTS

Chapter 1

邀請篇
Inviting

1 Accepting invitation
接受邀請

情境對話

Paul	I've got two tickets for the concert. Would you like to go? 我有兩張音樂會的票，你想不想去？
Helen	That sounds great! When is it? 聽起來很棒，是什麼時候的票？
Paul	May 24th at 7 P.M. 五月二十四號晚上七點。
Helen	Where do you want to meet? 我們要在哪裡碰面？
Paul	Let's meet in front of the library. 我們就約在圖書館前面。
Helen	Fine. What time? 好，幾點？

Paul	How about 6:30? Is it too early for you? 六點半怎麼樣？對你來說會不會太早？
Helen	No, not at all. 一點都不會。
Paul	Okay. See you then. 好，到時見嘍！

句型解析

◆詢問對方意見

(1) Would you like to go to the concert?

How about going to the concert?

Do you feel like going to the concert?

你想不想參加音樂會？

*feel like 表示「想要做某事；想要某物」的意思。

(2) That sounds great!

That's a good idea.

I'd love to.

聽起來很棒。/真是不錯的點子。/我很樂意。

(3) Let's meet in front of the library.

How about meeting in front of the library.

Why don't we meet in front of the library.

我們就約在圖書館前面見面。

(4) How about 6:30.

Let's say 6:30.

Is 6:30 O.K. for you?

六點半如何？

單字片語

☑	invite [ɪn'vaɪt]	邀請
☑	accept [ək'sɛpt]	接受
☑	concert ['kɑnsɚt]	音樂會
☑	library ['laɪ͵brɛrɪ]	圖書館
☑	not at all	一點也不
☑	See you then.	到時候見
☑	sounds great	聽起來很棒
☑	good idea	不錯的點子
☑	in front of	在～之前

2 Refusing invitation
婉拒對方的邀請

情境對話

Larry	There is a football game tomorrow at 6:00. Do you want to go? 明天六點有足球賽。你想不想去。
Jack	Oh, I really want to go, but I can't. I have to stay in and study. I'll have my mid-term exam the day after tomorrow. 喔，我真的很想去，但是我不能去。我必須在家裡唸書。我後天有期中考。
Larry	That's all right. Well, maybe some other time. 沒關係，嗯，那就另外找時間吧。
Jack	Anyway. Thank you for inviting me. 無論如何，謝謝你的邀請。

句型解析

◆表達意願

(1) Oh, I　really want to go, but I can't.

Oh, I'm sorry. I can't make it.

Oh, I'd love to, but I'm not free then.

Oh, I'm busy then.

我很想去，但是我不能去。

單字片語

☑ mid-term exam	期中考
☑ final exam	期末考
☑ the day after tomorrow	後天
☑ the day before yesterday	前天
☑ some other time	改天；另外找時間
☑ refuse [rɪˈfjuz]	拒絕
☑ football [ˈfʊtˌbɔl]	足球
☑ anyway [ˈɛnɪˌwe]	無論如何

3 Introducing yourself
自我介紹

情境對話

In a cocktail party 在一個雞尾酒宴會上

Robert	Hello, I'm Robert Dewitt. 哈囉，我是羅柏‧德威特。
Teresa	My name is Teresa Perkins. You can call me Terry. 我名叫特莉莎‧柏金斯。你可以叫我特莉。
Robert	Nice to meet you, Terry. 很高興認識你，特莉。
Teresa	Good to meet you. What do people call you? 很高興認識你，別人都怎麼稱呼你？
Robert	Bob. Please call me Bob. 包柏，請叫我包柏。

句型解析

◆見面時的問候語

(1) Nice to meet you.

Nice meeting you.

It's nice to meet you.

I'm very pleased to meet you.

I'm glad to meet you.

I'm delighted to meet you. (formal)

很高興認識(見到)你。

◆道別時的問候語

(2) Have a nice (good) day.

祝你有個愉快的一天。

Have a nice evening.

祝你有個愉快的夜晚。

Have a nice weekend.

祝你有個愉快的週末。

以下舉出一些常見的名字（ｎａｍｅ)及其暱稱
（nickname）：

男生名	
Name 名字	Nickname 暱稱
Albert	Al
Alexander	Alex
Andrew	Andy
David	Dave
Edward	Eddie/Ted
Joseph	Joe
Michael	Mike
Richard	Dick
Stephen	Steve
William	Bill/Willy

女生名	
Name 名字	Nickname 暱稱
Deborah	Debbie
Elizabeth	Liz/Betty
Jacqueline	Jackie
Jennifer	Jenny
Katherine	Kathy/Kate
Margaret	Maggie/Peggy
Martha	Patty
Susan	Sue
Teresa	Terry
Victoria	Vicky/Vicki

單字片語

☑ introduce [ˌɪntrəˈdjus]	介紹
☑ cocktail [ˈkɑkˌtel]	雞尾酒
☑ people [ˈpipl̩]	人們
☑ call [kɔl]	稱呼
☑ glad [glæd]	高興
☑ please　[pliz]	高興
☑ formal [ˈfɔrml̩]	正式
☑ weekend [ˈwikˈɛnd]	週末

4 Introducing two friends to know each other

介紹兩位朋友互相認識

情境對話

Nancy	Tom, this is my friend, Jenny. Jenny, I'd like you to meet Tom. Tom and I were colleagues before.
	湯姆，這是我的朋友珍妮。珍妮，我想介紹湯姆給你認識。湯姆和我以前是同事。
Jenny	Nice meeting you, Tom.
	很高興認識你，湯姆。
Tom	Nice to meet you, too, Jenny.
	我也很高興認識你，珍妮。

句型解析

◆介紹朋友給對方認識

I'd like you to meet (my friend) Tom.

Let me introduce (my friend) Tom.

I'd like to introduce you to Tom.

我想介紹(我朋友)湯姆給你認識。

小錦囊

1. 在美國，和他人第一次見面時，有幾個私人問題
   是不適合問的。若無意間脫口而出，會被認為是
   粗俗無禮的。

   例如：

   How old are you? 你幾歲？

   Are you married? 你結婚了嗎？

   How much do you earn? 你的待遇多少？

2. 當身處在美國時，必定會發現許多的culture shock
   (文化衝擊)。譬如說：當我們有機會到美國人家裡
   作客時，會發現當他們進入到屋內時，不會把鞋

子脫掉，而且絕大多數的美國房屋在屋內都鋪有地毯(carpet)。反之，在台灣，當我們到朋友家作客時，進入屋內必定脫掉鞋子，即使自己的襪子臭氣沖天，旁人還是得忍受這種痛苦的煎熬。

單字片語

☑ colleague ['kɑlig] = co-worker	同事
☑ friend　[frɛnd]	朋友
☑ each other	互相
☑ before　[bɪ'for]	以前

5 Running into an old friend

與老朋友不期而遇

情境對話

William	Hi. How have you been, Linda? 嗨，琳達，好久沒有你的消息，最近怎麼樣啊？
Linda	Wow, William. I can't believe it's you. What a coincidence! I haven't seen you for ages. You haven't changed a bit! 哇，威廉，我真不敢相信是你，好巧喔！我已經好久沒見到你了，你一點也沒變呢。
William	You don't look much different either. 你看起來也沒什麼變。
Linda	Are you still living in Dallas? 你還住在達拉斯嗎？

William	No, my wife and I moved to Chicago since 1996. 沒有，我和我太太自 1996 年就搬到芝加哥。
Linda	Oh, you're married? 喔，你結婚了啊？
William	Yeah, we've been married for two years and have a daughter. 對啊，我們結婚兩年了而且還有一個女兒。
Linda	By the way. Do you still keep in touch with Mike? 對了，你還有沒有和麥可聯絡？
William	Yes, we play tennis once a week. 有啊，我們每個星期打一次網球。
Linda	Oh, really? 喔，真的嗎？

William	Well, I'd better get going. Talk to you later.
	嗯,我該走了,下次再聊。
Linda	All right.
	好啊。

單字片語

☑ run into = come across = bump into	不期而遇
☑ coincidence [ko'ɪnsɪdəns]	巧合
☑ keep in touch with	保持聯繫
☑ lose touch with	失去聯繫
☑ change [tʃendʒ]	改變
☑ either ['iðɚ]	也是
☑ husband ['hʌzbənd]	丈夫
☑ marry ['mærɪ]	結婚

課後小點心

　　有的禮節(etiquette)，尤其在於無法接受他人之邀時，更應該給對方一種很願意接受邀請，但因為太忙、事先已經有約或是有其他更緊急的理由不得不拒絕。這樣會給予別人較為舒服的感覺。有時為了化解尷尬的氣氛，雙方都可以適時地補上這句話 "Maybe some other time./Maybe another time."。

　　另外，和別人約定時間後，就應當準時赴約，因為遲到總會讓約會變得掃興。當然，放鴿子的情形是絕對不能發生的。

Chapter 2

購物篇
Shopping

1 Looking around in a store

在店裡隨處看

情境對話

Clerk	Hi, may I help you? 嗨！需要幫忙嗎？
Customer	No, thanks. I'm just looking. 顧客：不用了，謝謝。我只是隨便逛逛。
Clerk	OK, let me know if you need some help. 好的，如果您需要幫忙，請告訴我。
Customer	Thank you. 謝謝。
Clerk	You're welcome. 不客氣。

句型解析

◆店員對顧客的問候語

(1) May I help you?

How can I help you?

What can I do for you?

Could I possibly help you?

我可以替您服務嗎？

◆回應店員的問候

(2) I'm just looking.

I'm just browsing.

我只是隨便逛逛。

單字片語

☑ looking around	到處看看
☑ store [stor]	商店
☑ possibly ['pɑsəblɪ]	可能
☑ You're welcome.	不用客氣
☑ browse [braʊz]	流覽；隨意觀看

2 At a fast-food restaurant

在速食店

情境對話

Clerk	Welcome to McDonald's. How can I help you? 歡迎光臨麥當勞，請問您需要什麼？
Customer	Yes. I'd like a cheeseburger, a milkshake and an order of large french fries. 我要一個起司漢堡，一杯奶昔和一包大薯。
Clerk	Something to drink? 要不要來點喝的？
Customer	No, thanks. 不用了，謝謝。
Clerk	For here or to go? 這裡吃還是帶走？

Customer	To go, please.
	帶走。

Clerk	That'll be $5.35.
	總共是五塊三毛五。

Customer	Here.
	錢在這兒。

Clerk	Here's your change, and your food will be ready in a few minutes.
	這是找您的零錢，您點的食物幾分鐘之內就會好。

Customer	OK.
	好的。

a few minutes later 幾分鐘後

Clerk	Here you are. Have a nice day.
	您的食物在這裡，祝您有個愉快的一天。

Customer	Same to you.
	你也是。

句型解析

◆常用的道別話

Have a nice day.

祝您有個愉快的一天。

Have a nice evening.

祝您有個愉快的夜晚。

Have a nice weekend.

祝您有個愉快的週末。

單字片語

☑ fast-food		速食
☑ restaurant ['rɛstərənt]		餐廳
☑ clerk [klɝk]		服務生
☑ customer ['kʌstəmə˞]		顧客
☑ cheeseburger ['tʃiz͵bɝgə˞]		起司漢堡

☑	milkshake　[ˌmɪlkˈʃek]	奶昔
☑	an order of	一客（食物）
☑	french fries	炸薯條
☑	change　[tʃendʒ]	零錢
☑	for here or to go	內用或帶走
☑	minute　[ˈmɪnɪt]	分鐘
☑	later　[ˈletɚ]	稍候
☑	same to you	你也是
☑	evening　[ˈivnɪŋ]	晚上

3 Grocery shopping
（雜貨店購物）

情境對話

Grocer	Yes, ma'am. What would you like? 是的，太太，您想買些什麼？
Customer	I'd like a pound of ground beef, please. 我想買一磅絞牛肉。
Grocer	Sure. Anything else? 好，還要其它的嗎？
Customer	Yes, half a pound of blue cheese. 要，再給我半磅的藍乳酪。
Grocer	Okay. That's a pound of ground beef and half a pound of blue cheese. Is that all? 好，您要一磅絞牛肉和半磅的藍乳酪。這樣就好了嗎？

Customer	Yes, that's it. 是的，這樣就夠了。

單字片語

☑ Grocery ['grosərɪ]	雜貨店	
☑ Grocer ['grosɚ]	雜貨商	
☑ ma'am [mæm] =madam ['mædəm]	太太；女士 （對婦女的恭敬稱呼） 夫人 , 太太 , 小姐	
☑ beef [bif]	牛肉	
☑ pound [paʊnd]	磅	
☑ half [hæf]	一半	
☑ ground beef	絞牛肉	
☑ blue cheese	藍乳酪	

☑ 另外有一種乳酪稱為 Swiss cheese（瑞士乳酪，其為一種淡黃色，帶大孔且味道不是太濃）。

4 Buying shoes

買鞋子

情境對話

Clerk	How can I help you? 我能替您服務嗎？
Customer	I'm looking for a pair of sandals. Do you have any suggestions? 我在找一雙涼鞋，你有沒有任何建議？
Clerk	How about a pair of these? 這一雙如何？
Customer	Let me try them on. 讓我試穿看看。

after a while 過一會兒後

Customer	These are a bit small. Could I try a larger size? 這一雙有點小，我可以試大一點的嗎？
Clerk	Certainly. Just a moment, please. 沒問題，請稍等。

a few minutes later 幾分鐘後

Clerk	Here you are. 您要的鞋子在這裏。

The customer tries them on. 顧客穿上鞋子後

Clerk	Do they fit? 合不合呢？
Customer	They fit perfectly. I'll take them. 剛剛好，我就買這雙了。

單字片語

☑ a pair of	一雙；一對；一副
☑ 使用 **a pair of** 的詞組有： a pair of sandals (shoes)	一雙涼鞋（鞋）
☑ sandals　['sændḷz]	涼鞋
☑ a pair of scissors　['sɪzəz]	一把剪刀
☑ a pair of gloves　[glʌvz]	一副手套
☑ a pair of trousers ['traʊzəz]	一條褲子
☑ try on	試穿
☑ fit [fɪt]	適合

5 Buying clothes
買衣服

情境對話

Clerk	We have a lot of nice sweaters on sale. Would you like to have a look at them? 我們有很多不錯的特價毛衣，您有興趣看一下嗎？
Customer	Sure. 當然有興趣。
Clerk	What size do you wear? 你穿多大尺寸的？
Customer	Medium. Do you have any in light blue? 中號的。你們有沒有淺藍色的？
Clerk	Yes, here you are. 有，就在這裡。

after putting it on 穿上之後

Clerk	It looks good on you. 這件毛衣穿在你身上蠻好看的。
Customer	Thanks. There's no price tag? How much is it? 謝謝。怎麼沒有看見標價呢？多少錢啊？
Clerk	It's $40. 美金四十元。
Customer	O.K. I'll take it. 好，我決定買了。

句 型 解析

◆誇讚對方

It looks good on you.

It fits you so beautifully!

它穿在你身上真好看。

單字片語

☑ on sale   大減價

☑ 要注意 on sale 和 for sale（待售）是不同的。

☑ 另外，提供減價拍賣時常見的用語：

everything must go	結束營業
final sale	最後特價
clearance sale	清倉大拍賣
last days of sale	倒數幾天特賣
big discounts	大減價

☑ T 恤或毛衣的尺寸大小：

small	(S) 小號
medium ['midɪəm]	(M) 中號
large	(L) 大號
extra-large	(XL) 特大號

☑ light blue
= sky blue   淺藍色

☑ dark blue
= navy blue   深藍色

☑ price tag   標價

6 Buying a car

買車

情境對話

Salesman	Can I help you? 我可以替您服務嗎？
Max	I'm thinking of trading in the car I'm driving now and buying a new one. 我正在考慮，將我現在開的這輛車賣掉，買一輛新的。
Salesman	Sure. We do take trade-ins. 沒問題，我們確實有提供折價，舊換新的服務。
Max	I just need a plain car. 我只需要一輛普通的車。
Salesman	We have a nice selection of compacts. 我們有一系列不錯的小型車。

Max	I would like a four-door compact, not a two-door.
	我要的是四門小型車，而不是兩門的。
Salesman	Are you looking for a manual or an automatic?
	你要找的是手排車還是自排車？
Max	An automatic.
	自排車。
Salesman	Are there any other features that you would like on the car?
	你還想在車上安裝什麼其他的配備？
Max	Yes, I'd like a stereo.
	我想有一個音響。
Salesman	We've got the perfect car for you right over here.
	我們這裡有一輛正適合您的車。
Max	Could I have a test drive?
	我可以試車嗎？

Salesman	**No problem.**
	沒問題。

小錦囊

在美國買二手貨品是很普遍的事，最常見的就是買二手車了， 原因不外乎是為了省錢。

常常聽到一些男生提到，在美國留學期間，若沒有車子代步，簡直是寸步難行，因為比起女性來說，男性若想要要求別人give a ride（搭便車）較為不容易。

以下是一個真實的例子，曾經有兩位男同學為了不想花錢請人送貨，又不願意三番兩次地麻煩朋友載他們，於是兩人便將床墊（mattress）從店裡扛回所住的地方，實在是精神可嘉。

單字片語

☑ trade-in		以舊換新
☑ plain [plen]		簡單的；樸素的；普通的
☑ selection [sə'lɛkʃən]		供挑選的同類商品
☑ compact [kəm'pækt]		小巧的
☑ compact car		小型汽車
☑ compact office		井然有序的小辦公室
☑ compact camera		精巧的袖珍照相機
☑ compact disc (CD)		雷射唱片
☑ manual		手排車
☑ automatic [ˌɔtə'mætɪk]		自排車
☑ feature [fitʃɚ]		特色
☑ stereo ['stɛrɪo]		立體音響
☑ test drive		試車

7 Paying

付款

Customer	How much is it? 多少錢？
Clerk	That comes to $12.25, please. 一共是 12.25 元。
Customer	Here is $20. 這裡是 20 元。
Clerk	Thank you. Your change is $7.75. Five, six, seven and seventy-five cents. 謝謝，找您的零錢是 7.75 元。五塊，六塊，七塊和七毛五。
Customer	Thanks. 謝了。

Clerk	Have a nice weekend.
	祝您有個愉快的週末。
Customer	You too.
	你也是。

單字片語

☑ pay [pe]		付款
☑ comes to		一共；結果
☑ cent [sɛnt]		分
☑ seventy [ˈsɛvn̩tɪ]		七十

8 Refund/Return/Exchange

退款 / 退貨 / 換取

情境對話

Clerk	Can I help you? 有需要服務嗎？
Bill	Yes, I want to exchange this skirt. It doesn't fit. It's too loose. 是的，我想換這件裙子，因為它不合身，太鬆了。
Clerk	Do you have the receipt? 你有沒有收據？
Bill	Yes, here it is. 有，在這裡。
Clerk	All right. Let me have this skirt. You can go over there and find the right size. Then come back and I'll make

the exchange for you.

好，把這件裙子交給我，你可以到那裡找適合你的尺寸。 然後再過來這裡，我會替您更換的。

Bill	Thanks a lot.
	非常感謝你。

小錦囊

在英美國家，如果對於所購買的商品不滿意（可能是物品損壞，大小不合，或是顏色並非自己想要的，理由為It's not the right size/style/color.），可以要求更換(exchange/replacement)商品或是退貨(return)，其實退貨也就等於是退款(refund)，此時通常必須附上收據(receipt)作為證明。

單字片語

☑ refund [rɪ'fʌnd]	退款
☑ return [rɪ'tɜn]	退貨
☑ exchange [ɪks'tʃendʒ]	交換
☑ skirt [skɜt]	裙子
☑ loose [lus]	鬆的

☑ receipt [rɪˈsit]	收據

☑ 其它可能要求更換的原因：

too tight [taɪt]	太緊
too big (large)	太大
too small	太小
too long	太長
too short	太短

課後小點心

　　當一般百貨公司或購物中心(shopping center)在大減價(on sale)時，消費者會有一種不買很可惜的心態，此時就會有很多人開始"血拼"，這和英文當中的"shop 'til you drop (不累不歸式的購物方法)"有異曲同工之妙。

　　購物是每個人在日常生活中不可或缺的一件大事，舉凡小到在速食店、超級市場、鞋店、服飾店，大到買車，處處可見購物時的對話。

　　當在購物時，店員最常對我們說的第一句話就是May I help you? 如果我們只是單純的window shopping (不購買只瀏覽櫥窗)，回答I'm just looking, thanks. 就可以了。但若是真想買一些物美價廉的商品回答Yes之外，相關問題的詢問及瞭解，就必須靠平時不斷累積的英文實力了。

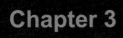

Chapter 3

外出辦事篇
Post office and bank

1 Buying stamps
買郵票

情境對話

Clerk	May I help you?
	我可以幫你嗎？
Amy	Yes, I need ten 32-cent stamps.
	可以的，我需要十張 32 分錢的郵票。
Clerk	Anything else?
	還要其他的嗎？
Amy	I also need five airmail stamps.
	我還需要五張航空郵件的郵票。
Clerk	Is that all?
	這樣就夠了嗎。
Amy	That's it.
	是的。

Clerk	All right. That will be $5.45, please.
	好，一共是五塊四毛五。

句型解析

◆詢問是否需要其它服務

(1) Anything else?

What else?

Will that be all?

Will there be anything else?

Is that all?

還需要其它的嗎？

◆告知價錢

(2) That will be $5.45.

It costs $5.45.

It comes to $5.45.

總共是5.45元

在美國購買郵票時，除了到郵局外，還可透過自動販賣機(vending machine)來取得，而購買的數量是以一本小冊子(booklet)為準，但也可零買。而在台灣，此種販賣郵票的機器目前很少到，然而在美國則處處可見其蹤跡，如機場及校園中。在郵票貼妥了之後，就必須去找郵筒投遞，但有些剛到美國的人居然找了半天，都找不到，原因是他們不知道郵筒長什麼樣子，還把郵筒誤認為垃圾筒，將垃圾丟進郵筒裡。

單字片語

☑ post office	郵局
☑ air-mail	航空郵件
☑ alright [ˈɔlˈraɪt]	好的
☑ else [ɛls]	其它
☑ cost [kɔst]	價值
☑ 32-cent stamps	32 分錢的郵票
☑ air-mail stamps	航空郵件的郵票

2 Sending a package
寄包裹

情境對話

Clerk	What can I do for you? 我能替你服務嗎？
Henry	I'd like to mail this package to New York. 我要將這個包裹寄到紐約。
Clerk	First class or parcel post? 你要寄 " 第一類郵件 " 還是 " 包裹郵遞 " ？
Henry	What is the difference? 有什麼差別呢？
Clerk	First class would be $8.50, and parcel post would be $2.25. 第一類郵件需要 8.50 元，而包裹郵遞則是 2.25 元。
Henry	How long will it take parcel post? 寄包裹郵遞要花多久的時間？

Clerk	About ten days.
	大概十天左右。
Henry	O.K. I'll send the package by parcel post.
	好吧，那我就用包裹郵遞來寄。

單字片語

☑ send [sɛnd]	郵寄
☑ New York	紐約
☑ difference ['dɪfərəns]	不同
☑ parcel ['pɑrsl̩]	包裹
☑ package ['pækɪdʒ]	包裹
☑ first class	第一類郵件
☑ second class	第二類郵件
☑ third class	第三類郵件
☑ fourth class	第四類郵件
☑ parcel post	包裹郵遞

3 Opening an account
開戶

情境對話

Customer	I would like to open a savings account. 我想開個存款帳戶。
Teller	A regular savings account? 普通存款帳戶嗎？
Customer	Yes. 是的。
Teller	Do you have any identification? 你有沒有任何身份證明文件？
Customer	Yes. Here it is. 有，就在這裡。
Teller	Great. Do you want the account to be in your name only? 太好了。你是不是只要以你的名義開戶？

Customer	No, I want a joint account for me and my sister.
	不，我想要以我和我妹妹的名義開一個聯合帳戶。
Teller	How much do you want to deposit today?
	你今天要先存多少錢？
Customer	$250.00.
	兩百五十美元。
Teller	All right.
	好的。

單字片語

☑ account [ə'kaʊnt]	帳戶
☑ regular ['rɛgjələ˞]	普通
☑ Here it is.	就在這裡。
☑ open an account	開戶

| ☑ | savings account | 存款帳戶 |

| ☑ | identification [aɪˌdɛntəfəˈkeʃən] | 身份證明文件 |

| ☑ | joint account | 聯合帳戶 |

| ☑ | 另外一種常見的帳戶為 checking account（支票存款帳戶） |

| ☑ | deposit [dɪˈpɑzɪt] | (v.) 儲存；存放
(n.) 存款 |

4 Using ATMs (Automatic Teller Machines)

使用提款機

情境對話

Joe	I don't know how to use the ATMs. Could you possibly help me? 我不知道如何使用提款機。你可以幫我嗎？
Sarah	Sure. First of all, insert your ATM card and enter your personal identification number. Then, choose a transaction. 沒問題。首先，插入你的提款卡，再輸入你的個人密碼。然後選擇交易方式。
Joe	I would like to withdraw $100. 我想要領一百元。

Sarah	O.K. Would you like another transaction? 好的。你還要執行其他交易嗎？
Joe	No, that's it. 不用了，這樣就好了。
Sarah	Now take out your card, cash and receipt. 現在拿出你的卡片，現金和交易明細。
Joe	Thank you for your help. 謝謝你的幫忙。
Sarah	You're welcome. 不客氣。

☑ ATMs = Automatic Teller Machines	自動櫃員機； 提款機
☑ insert [ɪnˈsɝt]	插入
☑ ATM card = cash card	提款卡
☑ personal [ˈpɝsn̩l̩]	私人；個人
☑ personal identification number	個人密碼
☑ transaction [trænˈzækʃən]	交易
☑ withdraw [wɪðˈdrɔ]	提款

5 Buying a money order
買匯票

情境對話

Clerk	Can I help you? 需要幫忙嗎？
Jim	Yes, I'd like a money order for $16.75. 我想買一張 16.75 元的匯票。
Clerk	Have you got an account with us? 你在我們這裡有沒有戶頭？
Jim	No, I don't. 沒有。
Clerk	There's a 50 cents charge. That's $17.25. 那要收取 5 毛錢的費用，所以總共是 17.25 元。

Jim	Here you are. 錢在這裡。
Clerk	Thank you. 謝謝。

單字片語

☑ money order		匯票
☑ account [əˈkaʊnt]		帳戶
☑ cent [sɛnt]		分
☑ charge [tʃɑrdʒ]		費用

6 Cashing a check
支票兌現

情境對話

Clerk	**May I help you?**
	我能替您效勞嗎？
Joyce	**I want to cash this check.**
	我想將這張支票兌換成現金。
Clerk	**Do you have an account here?**
	你在我們這裡有沒有戶頭？
Joyce	**No, I don't.**
	沒有。
Clerk	**There's a $2.00 charge. Do you have identification?**
	那要收取兩塊錢的費用。你有沒有身份證明文件？

Joyce	Yes, here's my driver's license. 有，這是我的駕照。
Clerk	Please sign the back of the check. That's $196.50. 20-40-60-80-100； 20-40-60-80-90-95-96 and 50 cents. 請在支票背面簽名。這裡是 196.50 元。 20, 40, 60, 80, 100；20, 40, 60, 80, 90, 95, 96 和 5 毛錢。
Joyce	Thank you. 謝謝。
Clerk	You're welcome. 不客氣。

小錦囊

That's $196.50. (這裡是196.50元。)

20-40-60-80-100；20-40-60-80-90-95-96 and 50 cents (5毛錢).

以上所列的例子為美國人算錢的一種方式。

* 在美國及一些其它國家，當銀行出納員或商店店員當面數錢（找零錢)給客人時，他們是採取累加的方式，而我們則習慣用扣減的方式。例如消費為15元，而拿出美金20元來找錢時，我們則用20減15為5元的算法。另外，我們通常也沒有當面，數零錢給對方的習慣，反倒是拿到錢的人自己會數。

單字片語

☑ cash a check	把支票兌換成現金
☑ driver's license	駕照
☑ sign [saɪn]	簽名

　　曾經聽過一個故事，一位上了年紀的婆婆，將辛苦一輩子的積蓄都藏在房裏的各個角落，等到她死後家人幫他整理遺物時，才發現房間裏到處都是婆婆的私房錢。因為在婆婆身處的那個年代，沒有像現在這樣發達的銀行業，她總會認為沒有將錢放在身邊，就會不安心。然而，在目前這個進步的社會中，銀行所提供的業務琳瑯滿目，而這些相關的會話用語是我們必須去接觸、去學習的，譬如如何使用自動提款機，如何用支票兌換現金等等。

　　除此之外，郵局也是我們常接觸的場所之一，像是買郵票、寄包裹、郵件等等。對了，順便一提，美國的自動櫃員機(ATMs)除了有取款的功能外，還有存款的服務，顧客不需在銀行內大排長龍。

　　另外，銀行對於開車的顧客還提供drive-through lane，也就是說不需下車也可以提領現金，十分省時方便。我們在台灣是否也見到此種外國文化的入侵呢？確實有的，像是麥當勞的得來速(drive-through)就是典型的例子。

　　因此，我們除了學語言的本身之外，該語言的文化背景更是不可不學。

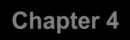

Chapter 4

休閒娛樂篇
Leisure and Entertainment

1 Seeing a movie

看電影

情境對話

Louis	Let's go to a movie. 我們去看電影吧。
Nancy	That sounds good. What's playing? 聽起來很不錯。現在上演些什麼呢？
Louis	There's a new movie called "The Enemy of the State." 有一部新的電影叫「全民公敵」。
Nancy	What kind of movie is it? 這是什麼樣的電影？
Louis	It looks like an action movie. 它看起來像是一部動作片。
Nancy	Oh, no. I hate action movies. 喔，不要，我痛恨動作片。

Louis	What about romances? Do you want to see "You've Got Mail" with Meg Ryan and Tom Hanks?
	那愛情片如何？你想不想看由梅格萊恩和湯姆漢克斯主演的「電子情書」。

Nancy	Yes, good idea! They both act well and it will be a box-office hit.
	耶！好主意。他們兩個演得都很好而且這部電影一定會大賣。

Louis	I couldn't agree with you more.
	我完全同意你的說法。

Nancy	What time does it start?
	這部片幾點開演？

Louis	There are shows at seven and nine.
	有七點和九點兩場。

Nancy	Let's go to the seven o'clock show.
	我們去看七點那一場。

Louis	All right.
	好啊。

句型解析

◆詢問播放的節目

(1) What's playing?

What's showing?

What's on?

在演(播)些什麼？

◆表示同意

(2) I couldn't agree with you more.

That's just what I was thinking.

That's exactly what I was thinking.

I feel the same way.

My feelings exactly.

我完全同意你的想(說)法。

單字片語

☑ action movie	動作片	
☑ romances	愛情片	

☑ 其他常見的電影類型還有：

literary film	文藝片
horror film	恐怖片
thriller film	驚悚片
detective film	偵探片
western	西部片

☑ box-office hit	票房大賣
☑ box office	售票處；票房
☑ hit [hɪt]	暢銷的；風靡一時的

2 Music

音樂

情境對話

Helen	What music are you listening to? 你在聽什麼音樂？
Tom	I'm listening to classical music. 我在聽古典音樂。
Helen	I don't know that you will listen to classical music! 看不出來，你會聽古典音樂！
Tom	It's nothing. I have got wild interest. I listen to everything. what about you? 那有什麼？我的興趣很廣泛，什麼都聽。那你呢？
Helen	I like pop music, especially love songs. 我喜歡流行樂，尤其是抒情歌曲。

Tom	Love songs are terrific, it seems to be girls' favorite. 抒情歌曲不錯，好像女孩子特別喜歡。
Helen	You bet. 沒錯。

小錦囊

　　在美國最受歡迎的音樂類型(musical styles)有以下幾類：

1. rock	搖滾
2. rap	饒舌
3. country	鄉村
4. pop	流行
5. classical	古典
6. jazz	爵士
7. gospel	福音

單字片語

☑ rock [rɑk]		搖滾
☑ rap [ræp]		饒舌
☑ country [ˈkʌntrɪ]		鄉村
☑ pop [pɑp]		流行
☑ classical [ˈklæsɪkl̩]		古典
☑ jazz [dʒæz]		爵士
☑ gospel [ˈgɑspl̩]		福音

3 In a restaurant

在餐廳

Hostess	Good evening, sir. How many people are there in your party? 先生，晚安。你們一共幾位？
Alan	A table for four, please. 一桌四個人。
Hostess	Do you have a reservation? 你有沒有訂位？
Alan	Yes. 有。
Hostess	May I have your name, please? 請問您貴姓？
Alan	Yes, it's Johnson. 強生。

Hostess	Smoking or non. 吸煙區還是非吸煙區？
Alan	Non-smoking. 非吸煙區。
Hostess	I'll show you to your table. Right this way, please. Will this table be fine? 我帶你們到座位上去，這邊請。這張桌子可以嗎？
Alan	This is just fine. Thank you. 很好，謝謝。
Hostess	Here's the menu. Please take your time. 這是菜單，請慢慢看。
Alan	Thanks. 謝了。

句型解析

◆詢問人數

(1) How many persons are there in your party?

How many persons (people), please?

你們一共有幾位？

◆告知人數

(2) A table for four.

A party for four.

(一桌)四個人。

◆指引方向

(3) Right this way, please.

This way, please.

Please come with me, please.

Follow me, please.

這邊請。

☑	guest [gɛst]	顧客
☑	party ['pɑrtɪ]	聚會
☑	reservation [ˌrɛzɚ'veʃən]	訂位
☑	smoking ['smokɪŋ]	吸煙
☑	non-smoking [nɑn 'smokɪŋ]	非吸煙
☑	menu ['mɛnju]	菜單
☑	person ['pɝsn̩]	人
☑	people ['pipl̩]	人
☑	follow ['fɑlo]	跟隨

4 Ordering dinner

點晚餐

情境對話

Waitress	Are you ready to order now? 準備好要點菜了嗎？
Alan	No, not yet. We need a little more time. 還沒，再給我們一點時間。
Waitress	O.K. I'll come back in a few minutes. 好，我幾分鐘過後再過來。

three minutes later 三分鐘過後

Waitress	May I take your order now? 我現在可以幫你們點餐了嗎？
Alan	Yes, we are ready. What's the specialty of the house? 可以，我們準備好了。你們的招牌菜是什麼？

Waitress	Shrimp Curry. 咖哩蝦。
Alan	It sounds good. I think I'll take that. 聽起來不錯，我想我就點這個嚕！
Friend 1	Same here. 我也是。
Friend 2	I'll have a medium Sirloin Steak. 我要一客五分熟的沙朗牛排。
Friend 3	A Roast Beef Sandwich for me, please. 請給我一份烤牛肉三明治。
Waitress	O.K. You'll have two Shrimp Curry, one Sirloin Steak, and one Roast Beef Sandwich. 好的，你們點了兩份加哩蝦、一客沙朗牛 排以及一份烤牛肉三明治。
Alan	Yes. 沒錯。

Waitress	Anything to drink? 需要喝的飲料嗎？
Friend 1	No, thanks. 不用了，謝謝。
Waitress	Just a moment, please. 請等一會兒。

句型解析

◆服務生詢問是否可以點餐

Are you ready to order (now)?

Would you like to order (now)?

May I take your order now?

Care to order now?

What would you like to order?

準備好要點菜了嗎？

單字片語

☑	speciality of the house	招牌菜；名菜
☑	speciality [ˌspɛʃɪˈælətɪ]	名產；特製品
☑	house	餐廳
	= restaurant	餐廳
☑	shrimp curry [ˈʃrɪmp ˈkɝɪ]	加哩蝦
☑	medium [ˈmidɪəm]	五分熟
☑	其它烹調方式有：	
	well-done	全熟
	medium-well	八分熟
	medium-rare	四分熟
	rare [rɛr]	三分熟
☑	sirloin steak [ˈsɝlɔɪn stek]	沙朗牛排
☑	roast beef	烤牛肉

5 Checking out

結帳

情境對話

Alan	Could you bring us the bill, please? 請把帳單帶給我。
Waitress	Just a moment, please. Your bill comes to US$60.25 請稍候，您的帳單一共是 60.25 元。
Alan	Do you accept traveler's checks? 你們收不收旅行支票？
Waitress	I'm sorry we don't honor traveler's checks here. 抱歉我們這裡不收旅行支票。
Alan	O.K. I'll pay in cash. 好吧！那我付現。

Waitress	Sir, here is your change.
	先生,這是您的零錢。
Alan	You may keep the change.
	不用找了。
Waitress	Thanks a lot. Have a nice evening.
	太感謝了,祝您有個愉快的夜晚。
Alan	You too.
	你也是。

單字片語

☑ check [tʃɛk]	支票
☑ bring [brɪŋ]	帶來
☑ bill [bɪl]	帳單
☑ accept [əkˈsɛpt]	接受
☑ traveler's checks	旅行支票
☑ honor [ˈɑnɚ]	榮幸,支付
☑ cash [kæʃ]	現金

6 Watching TV

看電視

Daniel
What's on TV tonight?
今天晚上電視上播什麼節目？

Bob
Let's see……Hey, there's a comedy on channel 26. I know you like funny movies.
讓我看看。嘿，第 26 頻道有一齣喜劇，我知道你喜歡有趣的電影。

Daniel
What's it called?
片名是什麼？

Bob
"There's something about Mary."
「哈啦瑪莉」。

Daniel
I have already seen that. What's on the sports channel tonight?
我已經看過那一部了。今晚的體育台在演什麼？

Bob	A football game.
	美式足球賽。
Daniel	Anything else?
	還有些什麼呢？
Bob	Well, there's a special about dinosaurs.
	嗯，有一個關於恐龍的特別節目。
Daniel	That might be interesting.
	那一定很有趣。
Daniel	Hurry! It is about to begin.
	快一點！馬上就開始了。

單字片語

☑ sports channel   運動頻道

☑ 其它不同種類的電視頻道：

    educational channel   教育頻道

    movie channel   電影頻道

musical program	音樂節目
news and weather	新聞與氣象
soap opera	連續劇
kid program	兒童節目，如
	Sesame Street（芝麻街）
variety show	綜藝節目
quiz show	猜謎節目
live show	現場節目

☑ sitcom = situation comedy　　電視喜劇片集；連續單元

喜劇（有若干基本角色和特定情境，而故事內容不同的喜劇）如

早期的 Three's Company（三人行）；Who's the boss？

（妙管家）；The Cosby Show（天才老爹）和最近的

Friends（六人行）都是大家所喜愛的節目。

　　歐美國家早已施行週休二日了，不用多說，他們所從事的假日休閒活動必定是應有盡有。有室內的，如看電影，聽音樂，或是家裏當個couch potato(成天守著電視不放的人)；還有一些戶外的活動，如各式的球類運動，觀賞球賽等等。

　　另外像是聽音樂、參觀美術館，到健身房workout一下，也是很棒的選擇喔！總之，作一些讓自己放鬆心情的事，就徹底達到休息的目的了，有時或許只是和朋友吃飯聊天而已。值得一提的是，在美國有些人會把洗車、清理自家的游泳池、除草或整理花圃當作是他們的休閒活動之一。

　　不過在台灣就很少有這樣難得的經驗了。

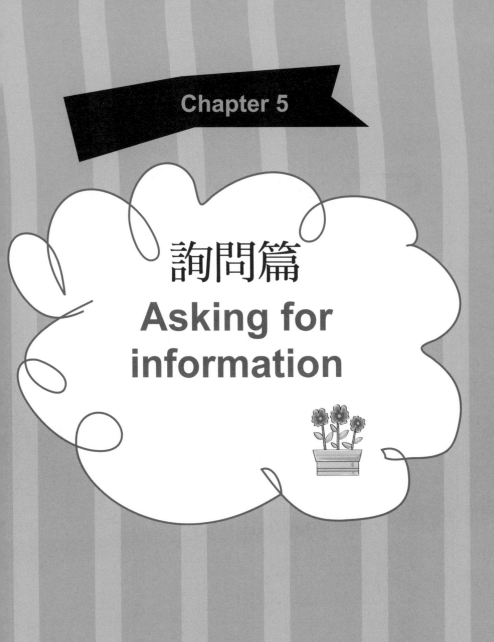

Chapter 5

詢問篇
Asking for
information

1 Asking for directions
問路

情境對話

Tourist	Excuse me. Could you tell me how to get to the Federal Building? 對不起，請問聯邦大樓怎麼走？
Julie	Go straight ahead for three blocks and turn right. It's on the right. 往前直走三個街區之後右轉，它在右邊。
Tourist	Did you say go straight ahead for three blocks and turn right? 你是說往前直走三個街區之後右轉嗎？
Julie	That's right 沒錯。
Tourist	Thanks a lot. 多謝了。

| Julie | You're welcome.
不用客氣。 |

句型解析

◆問路

(1) Could (Can) you tell me how to get to the Federal Building?

Do you know how to get to the Federal Building?

Could you tell me where the Federal Building is?

Do you know where the Federal Building is?

Is there a Federal Building near here?

請問聯邦大樓怎麼走嗎？

(2) That's right.

You're right.

Absolutely!

Definitely.

No doubt about it!

沒錯。

單字片語

☑ building ['bɪldɪŋ]	建築物	
☑ Federal Building	聯邦大樓	
☑ near [nɪr]	靠近	
☑ straight [stret]	筆直的（地）	
☑ ahead [ə'hɛd]	往前	
☑ block	街區	
☑ absolutely ['æbsə,lutlɪ]	絕對地；完全地	
☑ doubt [daʊt]	懷疑	

2 Asking for public facilities

詢問公共設施的方位

情境對話

A Excuse me, would you tell me where the (public) telephone is?

對不起，請問公用電話在那裡？

B There's one next to the men's room on the second floor.

在二樓男廁旁邊有一個。

A Thank you so much.

非常感謝。

B You bet.

不用客氣，應該的。

單字片語

☑ public facilities ['pʌblɪk fə'sɪlətɪz] 公共設施

☑ 當我們在百貨公司、購物商場 (shopping mall)、飯店、機場
等一些大型場所時，常常會詢問到下列公共設施的方位或地
點：

telephone ['tɛlə,fon]	電話
elevator ['ɛlə,vetɚ]	電梯
escalator ['ɛskə,letɚ]	手扶梯
main entrance	大(正)門
food court	美食街
exit	出口
parking lot	停車場
rest room	廁所
ladies' room	女廁
men's room	男廁
newsstand ['njuz,stænd]	書報攤
gift shop	禮品部
lost and found	失物招領處

3 Looking for a building
找建築物

情境對話

A	I'm looking for a stadium. Do you know where it is? 我在找一座體育館。你知道在那裡嗎？
B	No, I'm sorry I don't. I don't know this area very well. 抱歉，我不知道。我對這區域不太熟。
A	That's all right. Thanks anyway. 沒關係，總之還是謝謝你。

句型解析

◆表示自己不清楚

I'm sorry. I don't know.

I'm sorry. I'm not sure.

抱歉，我不知道。

單字片語

☑ stadium [ˈstedɪəm]	體育館
=gymnasium [dʒɪmˈmezɪəm]	
=gym [dʒɪm]	
☑ area [ˈɛrɪə]	地區；區域

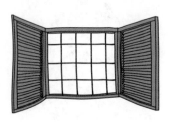

4 Looking for an apartment (On the phone)

找公寓（在電話中）

情境對話

Landlord	Hello? 哈囉？
Kelly	Hello. I'm calling about the apartment you advertised. Is it still available? 哈囉，我打電話詢問有關刊登出租公寓一事。目前仍然有空房嗎？
Landlord	Yes, it is. 是的。
Kelly	Could you tell me more about it? 可否提供我更多相關的資料。

Landlord	Sure. It's a one-bedroom apartment with a bathroom and a kitchen.
	當然，這是一個單人房的公寓附一間浴室和一個廚房。
Kelly	Great. How much is the rent?
	太棒了，那房租是多少錢呢？
Landlord	It's $350 a month including utilities.
	一個月 350 元含水電瓦斯費。
Kelly	How about the security deposit?
	押金需付多少？
Landlord	One month's rent. By the way, there is parking available. Do you have a car?
	一個月的房租錢。對了，這裡有附停車場，你有沒有車？
Kelly	Yes, but I'd rather walk to school. It's just a ten-minute walk, isn't it?
	有，但我寧可走路上學。走路只需十分鐘，不是嗎？

Landlord	Yeah, that's right.
	對，你說的沒錯。
Kelly	O.K. I'll go to take a look and find out more.
	好，我會過去看一下以便瞭解更多。
Landlord	See you then.
	到時候見嘍。

單字片語

☑ advertise [ˈædvɚˌtaɪz]	登廣告
☑ available [əˈveləbl̩]	可獲得的；可利用的
☑ one-bedroom apartment	單人房公寓
☑ utility [juˈtɪlətɪ]	水、電、瓦斯等公共設施
☑ security deposit	押金
☑ security [sɪˈkjʊrətɪ]	安全；擔保（品）
☑ deposit [dɪˈpazɪt]	押金

　　無論出國旅遊或是到異地唸書，對於新環境的不熟悉是理所當然的。這時大家就應該發揮愛迪生(Thomas Alva Edison)好學好問的精神。

　　曾經有一天，當愛迪生看到一隻鵝坐在牠的蛋上，於是問媽媽這是什麼原因？媽媽回答說：牠在孵蛋。他問：為什麼呢？媽媽說：為了要保持蛋的溫暖。

　　他又問：何謂孵化？媽媽說：孵化就是小鵝把蛋殼敲破然後從蛋裏跑出來。當天下午，他父親正在到處找他時，發現他竟然坐在鵝蛋上等待小鵝孵出來。結果如何，大一定都心知肚明了。

　　由以上的小故事得知，凡事想尋求問題的解決之道，必定得開口問，雖然不一定有自己想要的答案，但沒試過怎麼知道呢？何大多數人對於"問路"這種舉手之勞都會意幫忙的，況且這還是一次免費的對話機會呢！

Chapter 6

交通工具篇
Transportation

1 Car rentals

租車

Salesman	Hi. How can I help you? 嗨！我能替您服務嗎？
Bryan	Yes, I'd like to rent a car for this Saturday. 這個星期六我想租一部車。
Salesman	What's your price range? 您的租車預算是多少？
Bryan	Oh, from $30 to $45 a day. 喔，一天 30 塊到 45 塊。
Salesman	Well, we have a Toyota Corona. 嗯，我們有豐田 Corona 車型的車。
Bryan	How much is it? 這要多少錢呢？

Salesman	It's $35 for a weekend.
	週末一天要 35 元
Bryan	Is there any charge for mileage?
	里程數要另外收費嗎？
Salesman	No, there isn't.
	不用。
Bryan	Do you have something bigger than a Corona?
	你們有沒有比 Corona 要大一點的車子？
Salesman	Yes, we have a Lexus for $55. Or how about a Camry? It is only $40 for a weekend and no mileage charge as well.
	有，我們有收費 55 元的 Lexus。還是您要 Camry 這種車型的？週末一天只要 40 元，而且也不用加計里程數的費用。
Bryan	O.K. I'll take a Camry.
	好，那我就決定租 Camry 了。

單字片語

☑	price range	價格範圍
☑	charge	v. 收費 n. 費用
☑	mileage ['maɪlɪdʒ]	里程數

☑ Corona, Camry 和 Lexus 這三種車型都是 Toyota（豐田）公司生產的。Lexus 的價格最昂貴，再來是 Camry，較便宜的是 Corona，近年來，日本車在美國銷售情形十分良好，一般人認為日本車較為輕巧，省油而且在價格上還算合理。因此越來越多的人選擇日本車而捨棄美國車及德國車。

不過，近幾年已被「特斯拉」超車，「特斯拉」成為汽車市場上，最受大家青睞的車種。

2 By bus

搭公車

Maggie and Jane are at the bus stop 美姬和珍在公車站牌旁

Maggie	Which bus should we take?
	我們應該搭幾號公車？
Jane	We'll have to take bus number 34 first and transfer to number 10 at Palm Street.
	我們必須先搭 34 號公車，然後在棕櫚街轉 10 號公車。
Maggie	How much is the fare?
	車資是多少？
Jane	It's $1.25. Do you have the exact change?
	一塊兩毛五。你有沒有剛好的零錢？

Maggie	Yes. How often do the buses run?
	有。公車多久來一班？

Jane	The schedule says the number 34 bus comes every 20 minutes.
	時刻表上說 34 號公車 20 分鐘來一班。

Maggie	Hey, here comes the bus. I think it's the one we want.
	嘿，公車來了。我想這就是我們要搭的車了。

Jane	Get ready to get on.
	準備上車吧！

單字片語

☑ transfer [trænsˋfɝ]　　　　v. 轉乘 n. 轉乘券

☑ fare [fɛr]　　　　車資

☑ 在美國搭公車時，車資除了每次投現之外，也可以以較低的價格購買乘車證，稱之為 pass (乘車證)；如果需要轉車時，可以向司機索取轉乘券 (transfer ticket)，而此種轉乘券通常是免費的。

☑ exact change　　　　剛好的零錢

☑ schedule [ˋskɛdʒʊl]　　　　時刻表

3 By train

搭火車

情境對話

Traveler	What time is the next train to Boston? 下一班到波士頓的火車幾點出發？
Clerk	There's one at 8 o'clock. 八點有一班車。
Traveler	I'd like a round-trip ticket, please. 請給我一張來回票。
Clerk	All right. That comes to $20.50. 好，一共是 20.50 元。
Traveler	Which platform for the train? 我要到第幾月台搭車？
Clerk	Platform 2. 第二月台。

Traveler	Thank you.
	謝謝。

單字片語

☑ train [tren]	火車
☑ Boston [ˈbɔstn̩]	波士頓
☑ round-trip ticket	來回票
☑ one-way ticket	單程票
☑ platform [ˈplætˌfɔrm]	月台

4 By airplane

坐飛機

情境對話

Making a reservation 訂位

Airline agent	American Airlines. Can I help you?
	美國航空公司，有需要服務嗎？
Jim	Yes, would you please tell me about evening flights from Taipei to New York?
	有的，可否告訴我有關從台北到紐約的夜間班機？
Airline agent	Well, let me check.
	嗯，我查看看。

Airline agent	Yes, there's a flight at 8 P.M. 有，在晚上八點有一班班機。
Jim	Do you have earlier flights? 有沒有早一點的班機？
Airline agent	Yes, there's one at 6:30 P.M., but there's a stopover. 有，六點也有班機起飛，但中途必須停留。
Jim	Do I have to change planes? 需不需要換機？
Airline agent	No. 不用。
Jim	Okay, I'd like to make a reservation now. 好，那我就現在訂了。

單字片語

☑ flight [flaɪt]	班機
☑ stopover ['stɑ]	中途停留
☑ make a reservation	訂（機）位
☑ airline ['ɛr͵laɪn]	航線
☑ agent ['edʒənt]	代理人

5 Checking in
辦理登機手續

Airline agent	Good evening, sir. May I see your ticket, please? 您好（晚安），先生，可不可以看一下您的機票？
Jim	Yes. Here it is. 可以的，在這裡。
Airline agent	Do you have any luggage? 您有沒有行李？
Jim	Yes, I have two pieces. 有，我有兩件行李。

after a few minutes 幾分鐘後

Airline agent	OK. You're all set. Your gate number is 12. Go down this hallway and you'll see it on your right. 好，您的手續都辦妥了。您的登機門是十二號，朝這走廊往下走，您會看到它在您的右邊。
Jim	Thank you very much. 非常感謝你。
Airline agent	You bet. 不用客氣，應該的。

單字片語

☑ luggage [ˈlʌgɪdʒ]　　　　　　　　行李
= baggage [ˈbægɪdʒ]

☑ a piece of luggage (baggage) 一件行李

☑ You're all set.　　　　　　　您的手續都辦妥了。

☑ gate [get]		登機門
☑ hallway [ˈhɔlˌwe]		走廊；大廳；玄關
☑ You bet.		不用客氣，應該的。

課後小點心

　　美國各州視其情況而定，提供不同的大眾運輸工具。如地下鐵(subway)，是身處在紐約的人所不可或缺的一項重要交通工具。

　　在美國搭公車時可事先購買token(代幣)或是準備剛好的零錢，而這種代幣是和地鐵通用的。至於長途旅行，除了搭火車或Greyhound bus(灰狗巴士)外，自己開車或租車旅行也十分常見，目前有越來越多的人偏愛minivan，它不但可作為旅行的交通工具，平時上街購物時也是一個不錯的幫手。

　　當然，飛機的出現使得人與人之間的距離更為接近了，它更在許多人的生活中扮演著舉足輕重的角色。

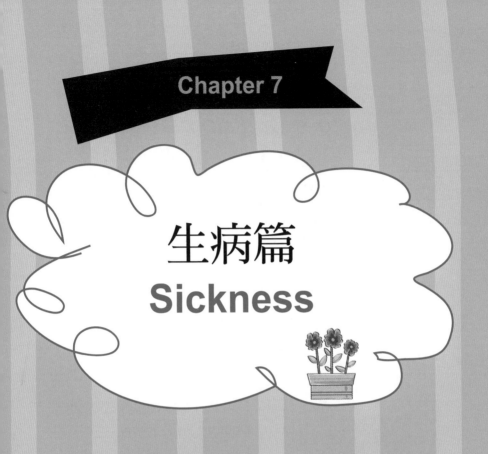

Chapter 7

生病篇
Sickness

1 Making an appointment to see a doctor (on the phone)

預約看醫生（在電話中）

情境對話

Receptionist	Dr. White's office. How can I help you? 懷特醫師辦公室。有什麼可以為您服務的嗎？
Mrs. Jones	Hello. Can I make an appointment to see Doctor White today? 哈囉，我可以和懷特醫師約今天看病嗎？
Receptionist	What's your name? 請問您的大名是？
Mrs. Jones	Karen Jones. 凱倫瓊斯。

Receptionist	What's the problem? 您是哪裡不舒服？
Mrs. Jones	I have a cold. 我感冒了。
Receptionist	Can you come on Monday morning at 10:00? 您星期一早上十點鐘可以過來嗎？
Mrs. Jones	Yes, I can. 可以。
Receptionist	Good. See you on Monday. 很好，那星期一見嘍！
Mrs. Jones	O.K. Thank you, bye. 好，謝謝，再見。

◆詢問對方目前的情況

What's the problem?

What's the matter (with you)?

Is anything (something) wrong?

What's wrong?

Is anything bothering you?

怎麼了？

單字片語

☑ make an appointment	約時間	
☑ see you+ 時間	～見	
例如：See you (on) Monday.	星期一見。	
See you on Monday morning.	星期一早上見。	
See you tomorrow.	明天見。	
See you next time.	下次見。	
☑ See you later.	再見。	
=See you soon.		
=See you around.		
☑ See you then.	到時候見。	

2 Seeing a doctor
看醫生

情境對話

Nurse	Hello, Mrs. Jones. Please have a seat. Do you have medical insurance? 哈囉，瓊斯太太，請坐，你有沒有醫療保險？
Mrs. Jones	Yes, I do. Here's my insurance card. 有，這是我的保險卡。
Nurse	Thank you. The doctor will be with you in a minute. 謝謝。醫師馬上就過來。
Mrs. Jones	Oh, good. 喔，好。

Doctor

So, Mrs. Jones…… what can I do for you?

瓊斯太太，有什麼能替您效勞的？

Mrs. Jones

I really don't feel well. I woke up with a terrible headache, a sore throat, and a fever.

我實在感到很不舒服。起床時頭痛得受不了，喉嚨也很痛，還有發燒的傾向。

a moment later 一分鐘後

Doctor

Well, Mrs. Jones, you have the flu. Nothing serious.

嗯，瓊斯太太，您患了流行性感冒。沒什麼嚴重的。

Mrs. Jones

What should I do now?

我現在該怎麼做呢？

Doctor	You should get some rest. Stay in bed for a few days and drink a lot of water. Here is a prescription for some medicine.
	你應該休息。在床上待幾天並喝大量的水。這是你的用藥處方。
Mrs. Jones	Thanks a lot.
	非常謝謝你。

句型解析

◆表示情況還好

Nothing serious.

　沒什麼嚴重的。

Nothing special.

　沒什麼特別的(不太好)。

單字片語

☑	terrible headache	嚴重的頭痛

☑ 其它以 **-ache** 為字尾的疾病
toothache	牙痛
backache	背痛
stomachache	胃痛；肚子痛
earache	耳痛

☑	sore throat	喉嚨痛

☑	fever	發燒

☑	flu [flu]	流行性感冒之省略

= influenza [ˌɪnflʊˈɛnzə]

☑ 其他健康問題及症狀：
cough [kɔf]	咳嗽
dizzy [ˈdɪzɪ]	頭暈
runny nose	流鼻水
stuffy nose	鼻塞
diarrhea [ˌdaɪəˈriə]	拉肚子；腹瀉
indigestion [ˌɪndəˈdʒɛstʃən]	消化不良
asthma [ˈæzmə]	氣喘
allergy [ˈælɚdʒɪ]	過敏

☑	prescription [prɪˈskrɪpʃən]	處方；藥方

3 At a drugstore

在藥局

情境對話

Mrs. Jones	Can you fill this prescription, please?
	你可以幫我依處方開藥嗎？
Pharmacist	Sure. It'll take about five minutes.
	沒問題。大概需要五分鐘的時間。
Mrs. Jones	Okay.
	好的。

five minutes later 五分鐘過後

Pharmacist	This is for your headache and fever. Take one capsule every four hours. This is for your sore throat. Take one teaspoon every four hours.
	這是治療你的頭痛以及發燒的。每四小時服一顆（膠囊）。而這是用來治療你喉嚨痛的毛病。每四小時服用一茶匙。

Mrs. Jones	All right.
	好的。
Pharmacist	That's $8.25.
	一共是八塊兩毛五
Mrs. Jones	Here you are.
	錢在這裡。
Pharmacist	Thank you.
	謝謝。

單字片語

☑ fill this prescription	依所需或指示來提供藥物
☑ capsule ['kæps!]	膠囊
☑ teaspoon ['ti,spun]	茶匙
☑ tablespoon ['tebl,spun]	大湯匙
☑ dessertspoon [dɪ'zɜt,spun]	點心匙
☑ soup spoon	湯匙

4 Having a motorcycle accident

發生摩托車意外事件

情境對話

Tony	How was your vacation?
	你的假期過得如何？

Jerry	Oh, not so good.
	喔，不太好。

Tony	What's the matter?
	怎麼了？

Jerry	I just had a motorcycle accident. I broke my ankle.
	我才剛發生了摩托車的意外事件，我摔傷了腳踝。

Tony	What happened?
	怎麼發生的？

Jerry	I went too fast round the corner and ran into a lamppost. 我轉彎的時候速度太快，撞到了路燈柱。
Tony	Did you go to the hospital? 你有沒有送醫治療？
Jerry	Yes, I did. An ambulance took me to the hospital. 有，有輛救護車把我送到醫院去。
Tony	Are you O.K. now? 你現在情況如何？
Jerry	I'm feeling better now. 我現在感覺比較好了。
Tony	You'll soon be fine again. 你會很快好起來。
Jerry	Thanks. 謝謝。

單字片語

☑ motorcycle [ˈmotɚˌsaɪkl̩]	摩托車
☑ accident [ˈæksədənt]	事故
☑ vacation [veˈdeʃən]	假期
☑ not so good	不太好
☑ broke my ankle	摔傷了腳踝
☑ ankle [ˈæŋkl̩]	腳踝
☑ corner [ˈkɔrnɚ]	轉角
☑ ran into	撞上
☑ hospital [ˈhɑspɪtl̩]	醫院
☑ lamppost [ˈlæmpˌpost]	路燈柱
☑ ambulance [ˈæmbjələns]	救護車

5 Seeing a dentist
看牙醫

情境對話

Dentist	What's wrong? 怎麼了？
David	I have a terrible toothache. 我的牙齒非常地痛。
Dentist	You may have a cavity. Let me check it. 你可能有蛀洞了，讓我檢查看看。
David	O.K. 好。
Dentist	I'll use a drill to remove the decay. 我將會用牙鑽清除蛀牙的蛀蝕部份。

after 10 minutes 十分鐘後

Dentist	You're all right now. 你現在沒什麼問題了。
David	Do I have to come back again? 我還要不要回來檢查？
Dentist	Yes. Let's make an appointment for the next time. How about next Wednesday morning at nine? 要，我們約一下下次看診的時間。下星期三早上九點如何？
David	No problem. I'll be here next Wednesday at nine. 沒問題，我下星期三早上九點會到這裡。

單字片語

☑ dentist ['dɛntɪst]	牙醫
☑ terrible ['tɛrəbḷ]	可怕的

☑ cavity ['kævətɪ]		蛀洞
☑ drill [drɪl]		牙鑽
☑ remove [rɪ'muv]		清除；去除
☑ decay [dɪ'ke]		齲齒；蛀牙
☑ appointment [ə'pɔɪntmənt]		約會

課後小點心

　　美國施行醫藥分業，醫師不提供藥品，病患必須持醫師的處方箋(prescription)到藥局(pharmacy)購買。

　　但像是一般的止痛或感冒藥，如Aspirin(阿斯匹靈)，Bufferin(百服寧)，Tylenol和Advil等，則不需要處方箋即可購得，這些藥品就稱之為over-the-counter medicines(不用處方箋的藥)。順便一提的是，在美國看病時，一定要事先預約，這幾乎已成了一種不成文規定。

　　在台灣雖慢慢地跟進，但還是有相當大的努力空間。

Chapter 8

打電話篇
Telephoning

1 One picks up the phone for oneself
被找的人親自接電話

情境對話

Mark	Hello. 哈囉。
Jerry	Hello, I'd like to speak to Mark, please. 哈囉，請幫我接馬克。
Mark	This is Mark. 我就是馬克。
Jerry	Hi, Mark. This is Jerry. 嗨，馬克，我是傑瑞。
Mark	Jerry? 傑瑞？

Jerry	Jerry Warton. 傑瑞瓦特。
Mark	Oh, Jerry! Hi, how are you? 喔，傑瑞！嗨，你好嗎？
Jerry	Pretty good. How about you? 我很好，你呢？
Mark	I'm just fine. 我也不錯。

句型解析

◆電話詢問句

(1) I'd like to speak to Mark, please.

　　Can I speak to Mark, please?

　　Is Mark there, please?

請問馬克在嗎？

(2) This is Mark.

Speaking.

我就是(馬克)。

單字片語

☑ pick up	接
☑ speaking ['spikɪŋ]	說話
☑ pretty ['prɪtɪ]	漂亮
☑ pretty good	很好
☑ How about you?	你呢？

2 One picks up the phone for someone

被找的人並未接電話

情境對話

Henry	Hello. 哈囉。
David	Hello. This is David. Is John there? 哈囉，我是大衛，請問約翰在嗎？
Henry	Yes, hang on a moment. 他在，請等一下。
David	Okay. 好的。
Henry	John, it's for you. 約翰，這是找你的電話。

talks to John ／和約翰講話

John	Who is it?
	是誰打來的？
Henry	It's David.
	是大衛。

句型解析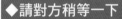

◆請對方稍等一下

Hang on a moment.

Just a minute/moment/second.

Just one moment.

Hold on a moment, please.

Hold the line, please.

Wait a second, please.

請等一下。

單字片語

☑ moment ['momənt]	瞬間；片刻
☑ Hang on a moment.	等一下。
☑ minute ['mɪnɪt]	分
☑ second ['sɛkənd]	秒，支持，第二的
☑ line [laɪn]	線條
☑ wait [wet]	等

3 **Wrong number**
打錯電話

情境對話

A	Hello. 哈囉
B	Hello, is Peter there? 哈囉，彼得在嗎？
A	Peter? 彼得？
B	Is this 2724-1188? 你那裡的電話是 2724-1188 嗎？
A	No. You got the wrong number. 不是，你打錯了。
B	I'm sorry. 抱歉。

A	That's okay.
	沒關係。

句型解析

◆不介意對方撥錯電話

(1) That's okay.

It's okay.

That's all right.

It's all right.

沒關係。

◆告知對方撥錯號碼

(2) You got the wrong number.

You have the wrong number.

你打錯電話了。

143

單字片語

☑ wrong [rɔŋ]		錯誤的
☑ sorry ['sɑrɪ]		抱歉
☑ got the wrong number		打錯電話了。

MP3-44

4 Leaving a message
留言

Laura	May I please speak to Jeff? 可以請傑夫聽電話嗎？
Tony	I'm afraid he isn't here right now. 抱歉，他現在不在。
Laura	Oh, I see. When will he be back? 喔，這樣子啊，他什麼時候回來？
Tony	He'll probably be back in an hour. May I ask who's calling? 他大概在一小時之內會回來。請問你哪裡找？
Laura	This is his friend Laura. 我是他的朋友蘿拉。

Tony	Do you want to leave a message?
	你要不要留話呢？
Laura	Yes. Please ask him to call me when he gets back.
	好，他回來時請他打電話給我。
Tony	Does he have your number?
	他有你的電話嗎？
Laura	No, he doesn't. My work number is 828-5300, extension 312, and my home number is 746-9725.
	沒有。我工作地點的電話是 828-5300，分機 312；家裡的電話是 746-9725。
Tony	All right. I'll give him the message.
	好的，我會留話給他。
Laura	Thank you.
	謝謝。

句型解析

◆要找的人不在

(1) I'm afraid he isn't here right now.

I'm sorry, but he's out at the moment.

抱歉，他現在不在。

◆問對方是否留話

(2) Do you want to leave a message?

Would you like to leave a message?

Can I take a message?

你要留話嗎？

單字片語

☑ message ['mɛsɪdʒ]	訊息
☑ probably ['prɑbəblɪ]	或許
☑ All right.	好的。
☑ afraid [ə'fred]	害怕的

5 Answering machine
答錄機

Terry is not at home and her answering machine is on
泰莉不在家，而她的答錄機響了

Hello. This is Terry. I'm not able to answer the phone right now. After the beep, please leave your name and number, and I'll get back to you as soon as I can.

哈囉，我是泰莉莎。我現在無法接聽您的電話，請在嗶聲之後留下您的姓名和電話，我會盡快和您聯絡。

單字片語

☑ machine [məˈʃɪn]	機器
☑ answering machine	答錄機
☑ beep [bip]	嗶的聲音
☑ as soon as I can	盡可能

6 Talking to an operator
與接線生對話

情境對話

Operator	Hello. 哈囉。
Fred	Hello, operator. I want to make a collect call to Taipei. 哈囉，接線生。我想打一通到台北的對方付費電話。
Operator	What's the number? 號碼是多少？
Fred	2711-4534. 2711-4534.
Operator	Whom would you like to speak to? 你想和誰通話？
Fred	Petty Brown. 佩蒂布朗。

Operator	Did you say Betty Brown?
	你是說貝蒂布朗嗎？
Fred	No. Petty Brown. "P" as in "Peter".
	不是，是佩蒂布朗。如同 "Peter" 中的字首 "P"。
Operator	All right. One moment, please.
	好，請稍候。

單字片語

☑ operator [ˈɑpəˌretɚ]　　　　　接線生

☑ make a collect call　　　　　打對方付費的電話

☑ collect call (對方付費的電話) 有分兩種：一種是 person-to-person (叫人的，如果非指定的人接電話不必付電話費)；另一種是 station-to-station (叫號的)。

☑ "P" as in "Peter"　　　　　如同 "Peter" 中的字首 "P"。

☑ 在英文當中，有幾個字母的發音單獨出現時，會和另一個字母產生難以區別的相似性，如字母 V, B, P, T 和 D。所以用 "Victor" 的 "V" 和 "boy" 的 "B" 來區分 "V" 和 "B" 在發音上的不同；在中文當中也有類似的情形，如古月 " 胡 " 和雙人 " 徐 "。

7 Directory assistance
查號台

情境對話

Operator	Directory Assistance. Can I help you? 查號台您好，有需要服務嗎？
Dale	Yes, I'd like the number of Paul Darby, please. 是的，我想查保羅達比的電話。
Operator	How do you spell the last name? 他的姓怎麼拼？
Dale	D-A-R-B-Y. D-A-R-B-Y。
Operator	Pardon. Did you say "B" or "D"? 對不起，你是說 "B" 還是 "D"？

Dale	"D" as in "Doctor". 如同 "Doctor" 中的字首 "D"。
Operator	One moment, please. 請稍等。

after five seconds 五秒鐘後

Operator	The number is 2732-0670. 他的電話號碼是 2732-0670。
Dale	Let me write it down. Thank you very much. 讓我寫下來。非常感謝。

小錦囊

在美國，若發生緊急事件(emergency)，如火災(fire)，尋求救護車(ambulance)或警察（police)支援時，必須打911，並非如台灣的119。由於現代科技的進步，手機現今已相當普遍，早已取代了呼叫器，現在的年輕人，可能都沒見過呼叫器了。

在這裡介紹幾種手機的説法：

cell phone

cellular phone

mobile phone

而呼叫器則為beeper或是pager，絕不是所謂的B.B.Call。若此B.B.Call的説法讓English Native speakers（以英文為母語的人)聽到了，一定會令他們感到一頭霧水。

單字片語

☑ directory [dəˈrɛktərɪ]		工商名錄
☑ assistance [əˈsɪstəns]		援助
☑ directory assistance		查號台
☑ pardon [ˈpɑrdn̩]		原諒
☑ last name		姓

課後小點心

　　大家一定知道電話是由誰發明的。沒錯，就是貝爾(Alexander Graham Bell)。因為貝爾的父親是一位語音學專家，耳濡目染地，貝爾從小對聲音就有興趣。之後，當貝爾有機會在學校教授失聰人士時，他便開始藉由機器試著幫助聾人去聽。於是這就激發起他利用電將人類的聲音由一處傳到另一處的想法。經過好幾年的努力，終於在1879年完成了這項偉大的發明。而當我們環顧周圍的各種發明時，不難發現很多新產物都是透過電話作為媒介的，如傳真機，E-mail等等。總之，Bell的發現改變了人類的生活，而他確實是一位功不可沒的大人物。

Chapter 1

Vacation
度假、休假

Unit

1. Vacation plans.
（度假計畫）

實用例句

- Let's go to Mexico for summer vacation.
  （暑假時，一起去墨西哥旅遊吧。）

- I am scheduled to take a 10-day vacation next month.
  （下個月我計劃休 10 天假。）

- I need a vacation. I am tired of working long hours.
  （我需要休個假，我厭倦了長時間的工作。）

- I wish I could take a trip to Disney World.
  （我希望能夠到迪士尼樂園去旅行。）

- What are our travel plans for this winter?
  （我們今年冬天計劃去哪裏旅行？）

實用會話

A Are you busy?
（你在忙嗎？）

B I am working on an assignment.
（我正在寫作業。）

Is there something you needed?
（你需要幫忙嗎？）

A Well, I want to talk about our vacation plans.
（我想跟你討論我們的旅遊計劃。）

B What about them?
（說來聽聽。）

We are going to Jamaica, right?
（我們要去牙買加，是吧？）

A Yes, but we need to plan where we will stay and what airline to use.
（是的，但我們需要計畫討論食宿與航班細節。）

B That's true.
（這倒是。）

Could we talk about it tomorrow?
（我們可以明天再討論這個嗎？）

A I would rather make the plans as soon as possible.
（如果可能，我想儘早做計畫。）

We might miss out on a better deal if we wait.
（如果等太久，可能會失去比較好的價格。）

B Okay.

（好吧。）

Let's talk about it now, then.
（那現在就來討論吧。）

A Great.

（太好了。）

I was thinking we could go online to check out airfares and hotel specials.
（我想我們可以上網查查，看看機票費用與住宿優惠。）

B Cool. We can use my laptop.

（太好了，我們可以用我的筆記型電腦來查。）

加強練習

➤ **Okay.**

A: We should quit arguing and come to an agreement.

B: Okay. What do you suggest we do then?

A：我們應該快達成協議，不要再爭論了。

B：好的，你建議我們該怎麼做。

> **Great.**

A: I have an idea for the project.

B: Great. Let's talk about it over lunch.

A：我對這個專案有個意見。

B：太好了，我們午餐時一起討論吧。

單字

vacation [vəˈkeʃən] ⓝ休假；假期

schedule [ˈskɛdʒʊl] ⓥ安排（時間）

tired [taɪrd] 疲倦的

trip [trɪp] 旅程；旅遊

plan [plæn] 計畫

possible [ˈpɑsəbl̩] ⓐ可能的

deal [dil] 交易

airfare [ˈɛrˌfɛr] 機票

agreement [əˈgrimənt] 協議；同意

suggest [səˈdʒɛst] 建議

quit [kwɪt] 終止

Unit 2. On vacation.

（休假）

- I love the beach.
  （我喜歡這海灘。）

- I am so glad we decided to vacation in Colorado.
  （我很高興我們決定去科羅拉多州度假。）

- Let's extend our vacation another day.
  （我們把假期多延一天吧。）

- Would you like to go sightseeing today?
  （你今天要去到處逛逛嗎？）

- I enjoyed our vacation this year.
  （我喜歡我們今年的假期。）

實用會話

A I am glad we chose a tropical place for our

160

vacation.

（我很高興我們選了到熱帶地區渡假。）

B Me, too.

（我也是。）

We can lie out in the sun all day.
（我們可以整天做陽光浴。）

A I am glad to be away from the winter weather in New York.

（我很高興可以躲開冬天的紐約。）

B I kind of miss home, though.

（但是我有些想家。）

A I don't. I don't want our vacation to end.

（我不會，我才不想結束休假呢。）

Let's stay a few more days.
（讓我們多待幾天吧！）

What do you say?
（你覺得呢？）

B Great idea!

（好主意。）

We can take a tour of the island.
（我們可以環島旅遊。）

A Fantastic!

（太棒了！）

I will call the tour agency.
（我來通知旅行社。）

B Okay.

（好的。）

But first, let's have lunch on the beach.
（但首先，我們先在海灘吃午餐吧。）

A That sounds like a great idea.

（這主意聽起來不錯。）

B We can talk about the tour while we eat.

（我們可以邊吃邊談。）

加強練習

> **Great idea!**

A: How about we go to the zoo on Saturday?

B: Great idea! I haven't been there in years.

A：週六去動物園逛逛如何？

B：太棒了！我好幾年沒去動物園了呢。

> **Fantastic!**

A: I got my first paycheck today.

B: Fantastic! Now you can go buy that new outfit you wanted.

　A：我今天第一次拿到薪水。

　B：太棒了！現在 你可以買你想要的新衣服了。

單字

beach [bitʃ] ⓝ 海濱

extend [ɪk'stɛnd]

sightsee ['saɪt'si] 觀光

tropical ['trɑpɪkl̩] 熱帶的

weather ['wɛðɚ] 天氣

miss [mɪs] ⓥ 想念

end [ɛnd] 結束

fantastic [fæn'tæstɪk] （口語）好極了；太美妙了

agency ['edʒənsɪ] ⓝ 代理商

zoo [zu] 動物園

Unit

3. Talking about the vacation

（玩回來後討論假期）

實用例句

- What was your favorite part of the trip?
  （這趟旅遊你最喜歡那一部份？）

- Did you see the fabulous photos of Gary's trip to Greece?
  （你有看過蓋瑞去希臘玩所拍的美麗照片嗎？）

- I can't wait to tell everyone about my vacation to Mexico.
  （我等不及告訴大家我的墨西哥之行。）

- I hope I remember to tell Mom about the cute antique shop I went to in France.
  （我希望能記得告訴我媽，有關法國那間古色古香的小店的事。）

- Bob told us that he saw a ghost while on his vacation in Spain.
  （鮑伯告訴我們他去西班牙渡假時遇到了鬼。）

實用會話

A I am glad to be back home.
（我很高興回到家了。）

B I am, too.
（我也是。）

I enjoyed our trip, but there is no place like home.
（我喜歡這次的旅行，但還是家最好。）

A Isn't that the truth!
（那句話再真實也不過了。）

Still, I didn't really want to leave that beautiful mountain cabin though.
（但我仍然不願離開那間漂亮的山間小木屋。）

B I'm going to miss hiking in the woods.
（我會想念在山林中健行的經驗。）

A I'm going to miss the peaceful streams.
（我會想念寧靜的小溪流。）

B Now we are back in the city with all of its noise and stress.
（現在我們又回到充滿噪音與壓力的城市。）

A That's okay.
（還好啦。）

It's home.
（畢竟是家嘛。）

B I know.
（我知道。）

I wouldn't trade it for the world.
（拿全世界來換，我也不換。）

A But it is good to get away from time to time.
（但有時出去走一走也不錯。）

B That's true.
（說的也是。）

I look forward to our next trip to the country.
（我期待下次到鄉下去旅遊。）

加強練習

> **Isn't that the truth!**

A: I hate it when people talk loudly on the subway.

B: Isn't that the truth! That is totally disrespectful to others.

A：我討厭在地鐵談話喧嘩的人。

B：這倒是真的，那樣做對他人很不禮貌。

> **That's okay.**

A: Do you want to go to the store with us?

B: That's okay. I was planning to go later on.

A：你要與我們一起去商店嗎？

B：沒關係，我本來要晚一點才會去。

單字

favorite [ˈfevərɪt] 最喜歡的

part [pɑrt] 部份

fabulous [ˈfæbjələs] 極好的；絕妙的

photo [ˈfoto] 相片

remember [rɪˈmɛmbɚ] 記得

antique [ænˈtik] 古董

ghost [gɔst] 鬼

back [bæk] 回來

cabin [ˈkæbɪn] 小木屋

hiking [ˈhaɪkɪŋ] 健行；長途步行

miss [mɪs] ⓥ 想念

woods [wʊdz] 森林

stream [strim] ⓝ 小溪；流水

noise [nɔɪz] 雜音；噪音

stress [strɛs] 壓力

trade [tred] 貿易；交易

disrespectful [ˌdɪsrɪˈspɛktfəl] 沒禮貌

totally [ˈtotl̩ɪ] 完全的

Unit 4.

Call in sick.

（請病假）

實用例句

- Josh called in sick today.
  （賈許打電話來請病假。）

- Ted calls in sick every other Friday.
  （泰德每兩星期的週五都會打電話請病假。）

- I can't call in sick. I used up all of my personal days.
  （我不能請病假，我已經把特休都用完了。）

- I am going to call in sick on Monday instead of using a vacation day.
  （我星期一打算請病假，而不用特休。）

- You should call in sick. You have a high fever.
  （你發高燒了，應該請病假。）

實用會話

A Have you seen Elsa?
（你有沒有看到愛沙？）

B She called in sick today.
（她今天請病假。）

A **Oh**. I hope she is feeling okay.
（喔，希望她快一點好起來。）

B Actually, she was sick yesterday, and she came in to work.
（事實上，她昨天就生病，但是仍然來上班。）

She felt worse and decided to go to the doctor.
（她覺得情況更嚴重了，所以決定去看醫生。）

A When is her doctor's appointment?
（她和醫師約什麼時候？）

B It was this morning.
（今天早上。）

The doctor ordered her to stay in bed for two days.
（醫師叮嚀她在家休息兩天。）

A **Wow.** I think I'll call her later to see how she's doing.
（哇，我想等一下打電話給她，看看她感覺如何。）

B That's a good idea. She is a good employee.
（好主意，她是個好員工。）

She never abuses her sick days.
（從不隨便請病假。）

A I know.
（我知道。）

When Elsa calls in sick, it is always something serious.
（當愛沙請假時，通常問題都很嚴重了。）

B We should send her a get-well card.
（我們應該寄張卡片給她，祝她早日康復。）

加強練習

➢ **Oh.**

A: Today, Bill came in to work 30 minutes late.

B: Oh. Yesterday, he was an hour late.

A：今天比爾上班遲到 30 分鐘。

B：喔，他昨天遲了 1 小時。

➢ **Wow.**

A: Did you know that Billy is back in town?

B: Wow. I haven't seen him in years.

A：你知道比爾已經回到城裏了嗎？

B：哇，我已經好幾年沒有見到他了。

單字

fever ['fivɚ] 發燒

worse [wɝs] 更糟的

decide [dɪ'saɪd] ⓥ 決定；判斷

appointment [ə'pɔɪntmənt] 約會；約定時間

order ['ɔrdɚ] ⓥ 命令

employee [,ɛmplɔɪ'ɪ] 雇員；員工

serious ['sɪrɪəs] 嚴重的

abuse [ə'bjuz] 濫用

Unit

5. Take some days off.

（休假幾天）

- I have accumulated 5 days off so far this year.
  （今年到現在我累積了 5 天假。）

- How many days off should I take?
  （我應該休幾天假呢？）

- I am going to request 3 days off to relax.
  （我將要休 3 天假，好好休息一下。）

- Billy took 2 days off to go visit his girlfriend.
  （比利休假兩天去看他女朋友。）

- Jessica is planning to take 4 days off to study for her college entrance exam.
  （傑西卡計劃要休假 4 天，準備大學入學考試。）

實用會話

A I have been working 50 hours a week for the

past month.

（過去整個月，我每週都工作 50 小時。）

B **Really?**

（真的嗎？）

You should take some days off.

（你應該要休息幾天。）

A I can't. I have to meet the project deadline.

（不行，我必須要截止日前把案子做好。）

B I think the boss will understand.

（我想老板會體諒的。）

You will be more effective if you take some time off.

（如果你休息，辦事會更有效率。）

A **That's true.**

（這倒是真的。）

Maybe I will request 2 days off next week.

（也許我下週該請假 2 天。）

I will have to postpone the project deadline three days if I take time off, though.

（如果我休假的話，案子的截止日就得往後延三天。）

B It's okay.

（還好啦。）

I think everyone will understand.
（我想大家都會體諒的。）

You are a hard worker and deserve a break.
（你工作很努力，應該休息一下。）

A Thanks.
（謝謝。）

I will make a formal request tomorrow.
（我明天將正式提出假單。）

B You will be glad you did.
（你這樣做是對的。）

A Do you have any suggestions for my days off?
（這幾天休假，你建議我去哪裡走走呢？）

B You should visit a spa and get a relaxation
treatment.
（你可以去泡 spa 作緩壓水療。）

加強練習

➤ **Really?**

A: I have to cancel our dinner plans.

B: Really? I am sorry to hear that.

　　A：我必須取消我們的晚餐計劃。

B：真的嗎？太可惜了。

➤ That's true.

A: We should keep our relationship professional since we are co-workers.

B: That's true. I am sorry for asking you out on a date.

A：既然我們是同事，就應該維持專業的關係。

B：這倒是真的，我不應該約你出去的。

單字

accumulate [əˈkjumjə͵let] 累積

request [rɪˈkwɛst] 要求

relax [rɪˈlæks] 放輕鬆

past [pæst] ⓐ過去的

really [ˈriəlɪ] 真的

project [ˈprɑdʒɛkt] 專案；企畫；學校研究作業

deadline [ˈdɛd͵laɪn] 截止日期

boss [bɔs] ⓝ 主管；老闆

understand [͵ʌndɚˈstænd] 瞭解；明白

effective [ɪˈfɛktɪv] ⓐ 有效的

postpone [postˈpon] ⓥ 延期

deserve [dɪˈzɝv] Ⓥ 應得的；得之無愧的

break [brek] Ⓝ 短暫的休息

formal [ˈfɔrml̩] ⓐ 正式的

suggestion [səˈdʒɛstʃən] 建議

relaxation [rɪlæksˈeʃən] 休息；放輕鬆

treatment [ˈtritmənt] 處理

cancel [ˈkænsl̩] Ⓥ 取消；中止

relationship [rɪˈleʃənˌʃɪp] 關係

professional [prəˈfɛʃənl̩] 專業的

Chapter 2

SOCIAL ACTIVITY
社交活動

Birthday Party

生日派對

實用例句

- Are you going to Jonathan's birthday party?
  （你要去強納生的生日派對嗎？）

- I am going to get Mandy a Barbie doll for her birthday.
  （我打算要去買芭比娃娃給嫚蒂當作生日禮物。）

- When is Ted's birthday party?
  （泰德的生日派對是什麼時候？）

- I hope John doesn't find out about his surprise birthday party.
  （我希望約翰不會發現他的驚喜生日派對。）

- Can you help me decorate for Pam's birthday party?
  （你可以幫我佈置潘的生日派對嗎？）

實用會話

A Timmy's birthday party is next week.
（提米的生日派對是下禮拜。）

Will you be able to come?
（你能參加嗎？）

B I don't know.
（我不確定。）

I am working late all next week.
（我下週整個星期都會工作到很晚。）

A What time are you getting off work?
（你幾點下班？）

B I am leaving at 10:00 pm
（我十點下班。）

Will that be too late?
（那會太晚嗎？）

A Well, the party starts at 8:00 p.m, but it will still be going on at 10:00 p.m.
（慶生會八點開始，但十點鐘時應該還持續著。）

B Wonderful.
（太好了。）

I will rush home from work and try to be at the party by 11:00 pm.
（下班後我會盡快趕回家，試著在十一點以前趕到慶生會。）

A You may miss the cake and punch.
（你可能會錯過蛋糕和水果酒。）

B **That's okay**.
（沒關係。）

At least I will still be able to give Timmy his gift.
（至少我可以把要給提米的禮物給他。）

A I will put you in the guest list then.
（那我就把你列在賓客名單上了。）

B Thanks a lot.
（謝啦！）

I will see you next week.
（下週見。）

加強練習

➤ **Wonderful**

A: Carmen is getting her braces off today.

B: Wonderful. I can't wait to see her beautiful new smile.

A：卡門今天要拆掉牙齒矯正器。

B：太好了，我等不及要看她美麗的笑容。

➤ That's okay

A: Can I help you shine your shoes?

B: That's okay. I am almost finished.

A：需要我幫你擦鞋子嗎？

B：沒關係，我幾乎快好了。

單字

birthday ['bɝθ,de] ⓝ 生日

surprise [sɚ'praɪz] 驚奇；驚喜

decorate ['dɛkə,ret] 裝飾

late [let] 很晚

wonderful ['wʌndɚfəl] 好棒的；絕妙的；好極了

rush [rʌʃ] 急著趕

gift [gɪft] 禮物

guest list 賓客名單

brace [bres] 牙齒矯正器

smile [smaɪl] 笑容

shine [ʃaɪn] 擦亮（皮鞋）

almost ['ɔl,most] ⓐⓓⓥ 幾乎

實用例句

- My sister's wedding is on Valentine's Day.
（我姐姐的婚禮在情人節那天。）

- When is Tim's wedding?
（提姆的婚禮是什麼時候？）

- I can't wait until my wedding day!
（我無法等到自己結婚的那天了。）

- I always cry at weddings.
（在婚禮中，我總會掉眼淚。）

- Judy is a hostess at Ann's wedding.
（茱蒂將在安妮的婚禮中擔任女招待。）

實用會話

A Hurry!
（快一點！）

We are going to be late for Molly's wedding.
（我們快趕不上茉莉的婚禮了。）

B **Gosh!**
（天啊！）

I am going as fast as I can.
（我已經儘可能地快了。）

A Well, move faster!
（那就再快一點！）

We have to be there in an hour!
（我們必須在一個小時內趕到。）

B I will be finished in ten minutes.
（我十分鐘內可以做好。）

Quit rushing me.
（不要再催我了。）

A **For goodness sake!**
（拜託！）

It takes an hour just to drive there.
（光開車到那兒，就要花上一個鐘頭。）

B Really?
（真的嗎？）

I though it was faster than that.
（我以為會少於一個鐘頭。）

A Nope.
（不是。）

That is why we must hurry.
（所以我們才得要快一點。）

B I understand.
（我瞭解了。）

I'll try to hurry.
（我會試著快一點。）

A As long as we leave soon, I think we'll be ok.
（只要我們趕快出發，應該就不會有問題。）

Weddings hardly ever begin on time.
（婚禮很少準時。）

I hope Molly is also running late.
（我希望茉莉也會遲到。）

B So do I.
（我也是。）

加強練習

> ### Gosh!

A: Gosh! Look at how fast that dog is running!
B: I know. He must be chasing something.

A：天啊！看看那隻狗跑的多快。

B： 我看到了，牠一定是在追什麼東西。

➤ For goodness sake!

A: Hurry up and finish you dinner.

B: For goodness sake! I just sat down to eat 2 minutes ago!

A：快點吃完你的晚餐。

B： 拜託！我兩分鐘前才剛剛坐下呢。

單字

wedding [ˈwɛdɪŋ] 婚禮

cry [kraɪ] 哭

hostess [ˈhostɪs] 女主人

sake [sek] ⓝ 緣故；理由

hurry [ˈhɝɪ] 匆忙；趕快

leave [liv] 離開

hardly [ˈhardlɪ] 幾乎不

chase [tʃes] 追逐

finish [ˈfɪnɪʃ] 完成

Unit

3.

Christmas Party

聖誕晚會

實用例句

• Does your office throw an annual Christmas party?
（你們公司每年有舉辦聖誕晚會嗎？）

• What are you taking to the Christmas party?
（你們都帶什麼去參加聖誕晚會？）

• I hate going to Christmas parties.
（我討厭參加聖誕晚會。）

• Will you please bring the eggnog for the Christmas party?
（聖誕晚會你可以帶蛋酒來嗎？）

• Will there be dancing at the school Christmas party?
（學校的聖誕晚會中可以跳舞嗎？）

A Would you be my date for the office Christmas party?

（我們公司的聖誕晚會，你可以當我的舞伴嗎？）

B I'd love to, but Jim already asked me.

（我很願意, 但吉姆已經約我了。）

A **That's cool.**

（那不錯啊。）

I guess I will go alone.

（我想我只好一個人去了。）

B Do you know Trisha?

（你認識泰瑞莎嗎？）

She needs a date.

（她需要一個舞伴。）

A I've only spoken to her a few times.

（我只跟她說過幾次話。）

She may not want to go with me.

（她也許不會想跟我一起去。）

B She mentioned that she was hoping you would ask her.

（她曾提過希望你能開口約她。）

She has a crush on you.
（她蠻喜歡你的。）

A Wow! I never knew.
（哇！我從來都不知道。）

B It's true.
（是真的。）

A Maybe I will give her a call tonight and ask her to the party.
（也許我今天晚上會打個電話給她，邀請她一起去舞會。）

B Sounds good. I think she'll be thrilled.
（聽起來不錯，我想她會很高興的。）

加強練習

> **That's cool.**

A: Matt went bungee jumping last night.

B: That's cool. I wish I were brave enough to go bungee jumping!

A：馬特昨晚去高空彈跳。

B：太棒了，我希望我也有足夠的勇氣去參加高空彈跳。

> **Wow!**

A: The police finally caught the serial killer.

B: Wow! I will feel safer now that he's been put in jail.

A：警察終於抓到那個連續殺人犯。

B：哇！他被關起來後，現在我可以放心了。

單字

annual ['ænjʊəl] 每年的

date [det] 舞伴

mention ['mɛnʃən] 提起；談及

crush [krʌʃ] （口語）熱戀

thrilled ['θrɪld] 非常興奮（thrill 的過去分詞）

brave [brev] 勇敢的

serial ['sɪrɪəl] 連續的

killer ['kɪlɚ] ⓝ 殺手

jail [dʒel] ⓝ 監獄

caught [kɔt] ⓥ 捕捉

finally ['faɪnḷɪ] 最終；終於

Unit

4. Farewell Party

（送別會）

- When is Peter's going away party?
（彼得的送別會是什麼時候？）

- I am sad that Tom is leaving, but at least I will see him one last time at the farewell party.
（湯姆要離開，我很難過，但至少我在告別聚會時，可以再見他一次。）

- I am throwing Mike a farewell party, and you are invited.
（我要幫麥克舉辦一個送別會，你可要來哦。）

- Has anyone seen the guest list for Kim's farewell party?
（有任何人看到金的送別會賓客名單嗎？）

- I can't go to George's going away party; I have a cold.
（我感冒了，所以無法參加喬治的送別會。）

實用會話

A Jake is leaving town for good.
（傑克要離開了。）

He got a job out-of-state, so we're throwing him a farewell party.
（他在別州找到工作，所以我們要替他舉辦一個送別會。）

B **How exciting!**
（好棒哦！）

I knew he had been looking for a career change.
（我知道他一直希望能夠變換職業跑道。）

When is the party?
（送別會是什麼時候？）

A The party is a week from today.
（送別會是下個禮拜的今天。）

Will you be able to attend?
（你會參加嗎？）

B **Of course!**
（當然！）

I wouldn't miss this party for the world!
（我絕對不會錯過這個聚會。）

A Jake is a good person.
（傑克是個好人。）

I am glad that he gets this chance at a better life.
（我很高興他有這個機會，可以過更好的生活。）

B Me, too.
（我也是。）

But I am sad that he is leaving.
（但他要離開，我很難過。）

At least we can have a nice party one last time to let him know how much we care about him.
（至少我們可以辦一次美好的聚會，讓他知道我們有多在乎他。）

A That's true.
（這倒是真的。）

Will you be able to bring something?
（你可以帶些東西來嗎？）

B I can buy something from the store.
（我可以去店裡買些東西。）

A That's fine.
（好。）

Anything will do.
（買什麼都可以。）

B I will bring a salad.
（我會帶沙拉。）

加強練習

> ## How exciting!

A: I am going to New York for summer vacation.

B: How exciting! New York is filled with fun things to do.

A：我要去紐約度暑假。

B：真是令人興奮！紐約有很多好玩的事情可以做。

> ## Of course!

A: Could you please cook dinner tonight?

B: Of course! I love to cook.

A：今晚你可以準備晚餐嗎？

B：當然，我很喜歡做菜。

單字

farewell [fɛr'wɛl] 告別

invite [ɪn'vaɪt] 邀請

cold [kold] ⓝ 感冒

career [kə'rɪr] (n)生涯規劃；事業

attend [ə'tɛnd] (v) 參加；出席

exciting [ɪk'saɪtɪŋ] 令人興奮的

cook [kʊk] (v) 烹調；煮

Unit

5. Go to see the fireworks

（去看煙火）

實用例句

- Let's go see the fireworks.
  （我們去看煙火吧！）

- Kim loves watching fireworks on Fourth of July.
  （金很喜歡在七月四號去看煙火。）

- Fireworks are illegal within the city limits. Let's drive to the country and see them.
  （在都市範圍內放煙火是不合法的，我們開車到鄉下去看吧。）

- Can Mike watch fireworks with us?
  （麥可能不能跟我們一起去看煙火？）

- We're having a fireworks-watching party. Would you like to come?
  （我們要辦一個煙火觀賞派對，你們想來嗎？）

A Do you like going to see fireworks?
（你們喜歡去看煙火嗎？）

B They are okay. I would rather watch them on T.V. though.
（還好。我比較喜歡看電視上的。）

A Oh, well, Sally has invited us to go see the fireworks display downtown.
（喔，好吧，莎麗邀請我們去看市中心的煙火表演。）

B Is that so? Well, I am going to pass.
（是這樣嗎？好吧，那我就不去了。）

I will just watch them on T.V.
（我看電視上的就好了。）

A It is a lot better to see them up close in person.
（親眼去看放煙火將是更棒的經驗。）

B I don't feel like going out this late at night.
（我不想這麼晚出去。）

A I understand.
（我瞭解。）

I will let Sally know.
（我會告知莎麗的。）

B **Thanks**.
（謝啦!）

I think I might actually just go to bed early.
（事實上，我想我可能會早點睡覺。）

A What about the fireworks?
（那煙火表演呢？）

B I will record the news tonight and watch them on T.V. tomorrow.
（我會把今晚的夜間新聞錄下來，明天再放來看。）

加強練習

➢ **Is that so?**

A: Julie broke her leg yesterday.

B: Is that so? I heard she sprained her ankle.

A：茱麗昨天摔斷了腿。

B：是嗎？我聽說她扭傷了腳踝。

➢ **Thanks.**

A: I will give Suzy the message.

B: Thanks. I hope she understands.

A：我會把這個訊息告知蘇茜的。

B：謝啦。我希望她能瞭解。

firework [ˈfaɪrwɝk] 煙火

illegal [ɪˈligl̩] ⓐ 不法的；非法

limit [ˈlɪmɪt] ⓝ 界限；範圍

country [ˈkʌntrɪ] ⓝ鄉下

display [dɪsˈple] 展示；陳列

downtown [ˈdaʊnˈtaʊn] 市區；市中心

pass [pæs] 不參加

record [rɪˈkɔrd] ⓥ 錄影

sprain [spren] 扭傷

ankle [ˈæŋkl̩] 腳踝

message [ˈmɛsɪdʒ] 留言；訊息

Unit

6. Go on picnics

（去野餐）

實用例句

- What should I bring to tomorrow's picnic?
  （明天野餐我該帶些什麼？）

- Are you going camping this weekend?
  （你這個週末要去露營嗎？）

- I don't like camping because of all of the insects.
  （我不喜歡露營，因為會碰到很多種類的昆蟲。）

- Today is great weather for a picnic.
  （今天是個野餐的好天氣。）

- I would like for you to come to our monthly picnic next week.
  （我想邀請你下週來參加我們每月舉辦的野餐。）

A Today is a great day for a picnic.
（今天是個野餐的好日子。）

B I know. The weather is nice and warm.
（我知道，因為天氣又好又　　。）

A Let's have a picnic lunch in the park.
（一起去在公園野餐吧！）

B That's a great idea.
（那是個好主意。）

What should we take?
（我們該帶什麼呢？）

A We can take sandwiches, chips, and soda.
（我們可以帶些三明治、餅乾和沙拉。）

But what should we take for dessert?
（但甜點要帶些什麼呢？）

B How about watermelon?
（帶西瓜怎麼樣？）

A **Awesome.**
（太好了！）

This will be a nice picnic.
（這將是個美好的野餐。）

B We can also take our bikes and ride along the trail.

（我們也可以帶腳踏車延著路騎。）

A Fantastic!

（太棒了！）

We can get some much-needed exercise.
（我們可以得到我們欠缺的運動量。）

B This is going to be so much fun!
（這一定會很好玩的。）

加強練習

> ## Awesome

A: Julie and Jamie both made the swim team.

B: Awesome! They both deserved to make it.

A：茱麗和潔咪都加入了游泳校隊。

B：太好了！那是她們應得的。

> ## Fantastic

A: I made reservations for us at the Olive Garden.

B: Fantastic. I have been craving pasta all week.

A：我在橄欖花園訂了位。

B：太棒了！我想吃義大利麵已經想了一整個禮拜了。

單字

picnic ['pɪknɪk] 野餐

insect ['ɪnsɛkt] ⓝ 昆蟲

camp [kæmp] ⓝ 營區；ⓥ 露營

monthly ['mʌnθlɪ] 每月的

park [pɑrk] 公園

dessert [dɪ'zɝt] ⓝ（飯後）甜點

awesome ['ɔsəm]（口語）很棒的

trail [trel] 路徑

fantastic [fæn'tæstɪk]（口語）好極了；太美妙了

exercise ['ɛksɚ,saɪz] 運動

reservation [,rɛzɚ'veʃən] 預訂

Chapter 3

HOBBY/SPORTS

嗜好和運動

Unit

1. Playing basketball

（打籃球）

實用例句

- I play basketball for an hour every day for exercise.
  （我每天打籃球一個小時當作運動。）

- How long have you been playing basketball?
  （你籃球打了多久？）

- I made the school varsity basketball team.
  （我參加了大學校際籃球隊。）

- Let's go to the park and play basketball.
  （我們一起去公園打籃球吧！）

- Molly, would you like to join our basketball club?
  （茉莉，妳想加入我們籃球俱樂部嗎？）

實用會話

A Hey, did Jamie ever make it to the basketball game?

（嗨，傑咪有機會打籃球嗎？）

B No, she had to go in to work early.

（不，她必須很早上班。）

A **How awful!**

（這真是太糟了！）

They are always making her go in to work early.

（他們總是叫她很早去上班。）

B We just played a second game later on that night when she got off work.

（當她晚上下班後，我們才進行第二場賽。）

It was a lot of fun.

（真的很好玩。）

You should play with us next time.

（下次，你應該跟我們一起打。）

A Sure! That sounds like fun.

（當然，聽起來很有意思。）

When are you guys getting together again for a game?

（你們下次碰面玩球是什麼時候？）

B We will probably meet on Sunday afternoon.

（可能是星期天下午吧。）

A That would be a great time for me.

（這時間對我來說剛好。）

B **Terrific.**

（太好了！）

We are planning to play for a couple of hours.
（我們計畫要打好幾個鐘頭。）

A Okay. I will bring plenty of water.

（好，我會帶足夠的水來。）

B You'll need it.

（你會需要的。）

We plan to work up a sweat.
（我們計畫要流很多汗。）

加強練習

> ## How awful!

A: Jane slipped and fell in the mud today.

B: How awful! Is she hurt?

A：今天珍滑倒在泥巴裡。

B：真糟糕，她有受傷嗎？

➢ Terrific.

A: I am getting married!

B: Terrific! When did he propose?

A：我要結婚了。

B：太棒了！他什麼時候求婚的？

單字

exercise [ˈɛksəˌsaɪz] 運動

basketball [ˈbæskɪtˌbɔl] ⓝ 籃球

team [tim] 隊伍；團隊

join [dʒɔɪn] 加入

fun [fʌn] 好玩；樂趣

terrific [təˈrɪfɪk] 很好的

sweat [swɛt] 流汗

mud [mʌd] 泥巴

hurt [hɝt] 痛；傷害

propose [prəˈpoz] 求婚

Playing soccer

（踢足球）

實用例句

- Soccer is a difficult sport.
  （足球是一個困難的運動。）

- Peter plays soccer three times a week.
  （彼得一週踢三次足球。）

- I am dedicated to increasing my skill as a
  soccer player.
  （我認真要改善自己身為足球員的技巧。）

- Does Jan play soccer?
  （珍踢足球嗎？）

- I am trying out for the city soccer league.
  （我想試著加入都會足球聯盟。）

實用會話

A I am going to a soccer game today.

（今天我要去看足球賽。）

B Really?

（真的？）

Could I go too?

（我可以一起去嗎？）

A Well, I already bought my ticket.

（可是我已經買好票了。）

You might be able to buy a ticket at the gate.

（你可能可以在入口處買門票。）

B Would I be able to sit with you?

（我會和你坐在一起嗎？）

A Yes. It is general admission.

（可以，那是不劃位的票。）

B **Great.**

（太好了！）

I will call the ticket office to see if they are still selling tickets.

（我會打電話去售票辦公室，問是否仍有售票。）

I love soccer.

（我熱愛足球。）

A I do, too.

（我也是。）

I have been playing since I was five.
（我從五歲大時就開始玩足球。）

B I don't play, but I love to watch.

（我不玩足球，但喜歡看足球賽。）

A It's a great sport.

（那是個很棒的運動。）

There is a lot of skill involved.
（需要許多技巧。）

B I know.

（我知道。）

That's why I appreciate the game so much.
（這是為什麼我很喜歡觀賞球賽的原因。）

加強練習

> **Great**

A: I reached my weight loss goal.

B: Great. I knew you could do it.

　　A：我達到減重目標了。

　　B：太好了，我就知道你辦得到。

> ## I know

A: Maria won't be in for work today.

B: I know. She called me and left a message.

　　A：瑪麗亞今天不會來上班。

　　B：我知道，她有打電話留言給我。

單字

difficult [ˈdɪfəˌkʌlt] ⓐ 困難的

soccer [ˈsɑkɚ] 足球

dedicated [ˈdɛdɪˌketɪd] 一心一意的；專注的；很投入的

increase [ɪnˈkris] 增加；增強

skill [skɪl] 技巧

league [lig] 聯盟

general [ˈdʒɛnərəl] 一般的

admission [ədˈmɪʃən] ⓝ 准予入場

involve [ɪnˈvɑlv] 牽涉

appreciate [əˈpriʃɪˌet] ⓥ 鑑賞；感激

goal [gol] 目標

Collecting coins

（收集硬幣）

實用例句

• I have been collecting coins for 10 years.
（我已經收集硬幣十年了。）

• Todd has coins from all over the world.
（陶德有全世界各地方的硬幣。）

• Travis is starting a coin-collecting club.
（崔維斯將要成立一個硬幣收集俱樂部。）

• I have over 100 coins in my collection.
（我的硬幣收藏超過一百。）

• Could you help me start my own coin collection?
（你可以幫我開始我個人的硬幣收集嗎？）

實用會話

A James went to the coin collecting convention.

（詹姆士去硬幣收集大會了。）

B How long has he been collecting coins?
（他收集硬幣多久了？）

A He has been a collector for about 15 years.
（他是十五年的收藏家了。）

B **How interesting!**
（好有趣喔！）

Do you know what made him start that hobby?
（你知道是什麼原因，讓他開始這個興趣的嗎？）

A I believe his father got him interested in it.
（我想是他爸爸讓他產生興趣的。）

His dad owns a coin shop.
（他爸爸有一間硬幣店。）

B Wow! What an interesting hobby.
（哇！好有趣的嗜好！）

I should ask him if some of my old coins are worth anything.
（我應該問他，看看我的一些舊硬幣是否有價值。）

A You should do that.
（你應該那樣做。）

He is pretty accurate at valuing old coins.
（他對於舊硬幣的價值很有概念。）

B Do you know how much his collection is worth?

（你知道他的收藏有多少價值？）

A His collection is valued at $100,000.

（他的收集值十萬美金。）

B **Oh, my!** That's impressive.

（天啊！真是讓人印象深刻。）

加強練習

➢ How interesting!

A: On the field trip, we looked at fossils!

B: How interesting! I wish I could have gone, too.

A：在這次旅行中，我們觀賞了化石。

B：好有趣！ 真希望我也有去。

➢ Oh, my!

A: Oh, my! That little girl just tripped and fell over.

B: Oh, no! I hope she's ok.

A：天啊！那個小女孩被絆了一下、跌倒了。

B：喔！不！ 希望她沒事。

單字

collect [kə'lɛkt] ⓥ 收集

coin [kɔɪn] 硬幣

collection [kə'lɛkʃən] 精品系列;收藏品

convention [kən'vɛnʃən] 集會

hobby ['hɑbɪ] 嗜好

own [on] ⓝ擁有

accurate ['ækjə,rɪt] 準確的

value ['vælju] ⓥ 估價

worth [wɝθ] 價值

impressive [ɪm'prɛsɪv] 印象深刻的

fossil ['fɑsḷ] 化石

4. Playing the piano

（彈鋼琴）

實用例句

- How long does it take to be a great pianist?
  （成為一個成功的鋼琴家要花多久時間？）

- I practice piano every day for two hours.
  （我每天練二小時鋼琴。）

- Stella has been playing the piano since she was three years old.
  （史黛拉從三歲就開始彈鋼琴了。）

- I started taking piano lessons last month.
  （上個月我開始上鋼琴課。）

- Can you show me how to play the piano?
  （你可以告訴我如何彈鋼琴嗎？）

實用會話

A I get tired of practicing the piano.

（我對於練鋼琴感到厭煩。）

B But you are such a good pianist.

（但你是很棒的鋼琴家啊。）

A I have to practice 2 hours a day.

（我必須每天練習二小時。）

B You will appreciate it later on.

（將來你會感謝這種練習的。）

A You're probably right.

（你也許是對的。）

Sometimes I just wish I could do other things instead of practice.

（有時候我只希望可以做做其他的事，而不只是一直練習。）

B I understand. When you get older, you can still have piano as a hobby.

（我瞭解。當你再年長一些，你仍可以把鋼琴當作嗜好。）

A That's true.

（那倒是真的。）

I guess I will suffer through practice until I can appreciate playing more.

（我想我會繼續忍耐，直到自己可以領悟演奏的樂趣。）

B Good choice.

（好選擇！）

Maybe you could practice in thirty-minute
intervals instead of two-hour intervals.
（也許你可以每次練習半小時，而不是一次練習兩小時。）

A That's a great idea.
（那是個好主意。）

That would make it easier for me to deal with.
（這樣對我來說容易多了。）

B Well, good luck with your practicing.
（好吧！祝你練習順利。）

加強練習

➤ That's true.

A: Billy should focus more on schoolwork.

B: That's true. I rarely see him study.

A：比利應該多專注在學校課程上。

B：這倒是真的，我很少看到他在念書。

➤ Good choice.

A: I think I will take a music appreciation class
next semester.

B: Good choice. I learned a lot when I took
that class.

A：我想我下學期會上一門音樂欣賞課程。

B：好選擇。當我在上那門課時，學到很多東西。

單字

pianist [pɪ'ænɪst] 鋼琴家

practice ['præktɪs] 練習

probably ['prɑbəblɪ] 或許；可能的

suffer ['sʌfɚ] ⓥ 遭難；受苦

interval ['ɪntɚvl̩] 間隔

rarely ['rɛrlɪ] 不常；難得的

focus ['fokəs] 專注

appreciation [əpriʃɪ'eʃən] 欣賞

Unit

5. Playing volleyball
（玩排球）

實用例句

- Jenny is a great volleyball player.
  （珍妮是一個優秀的排球員。）

- Would you like to go to the beach and play a game of volleyball?
  （你想要去海邊，玩沙灘排球嗎？）

- I have been playing volleyball for years.
  （我玩排球已經好多年了。）

- Volleyball is a great way to stay in shape.
  （玩排球是一個保持身材的好方法。）

- Playing volleyball helps develop hand-eye coordination.
  （玩排球幫助人們發展手眼協調能力。）

實用會話

A Volleyball is not my best sport, but I really enjoy playing it.

（排球不是我最擅長的運動，但我真的很喜歡打排球。）

B Yeah. It's a good way to get exercise.

（是啊，那是個好的運動方式。）

A Well, it builds hand-eye coordination, but I don't see how you get that much exercise.

（是的，它培養手眼協調能力，但我看不出來打排球可以有那麼多的運動量。）

There isn't a lot of running or moving involved.

（打排球不用大幅度的跑步或移動。）

B That's true. But it takes speed to run and hit the ball over the net.

（那倒是真的，但打排球需要跑的很快，把球打過中線。）

All of that running can give you quite a workout.

（這些跑步都可帶給你相當的運動。）

A In all of my years of playing volleyball, I find that it doesn't really give me a good workout.

（在我打排球的這些年，我發現它沒有真正讓我運動到。）

B Well, let's agree to disagree.

（好吧，該我們同意各人可以有不同的意見吧。）

輕鬆打開英語話匣子

合著／蘇盈盈・Lily Thomas
責任編輯／Lilibet Chang
封面設計／李秀英
內文排版／Lin Lin House
出版者／哈福企業有限公司
地址／新北市板橋區五權街16 號 1 樓
電話／ (02) 2808-4587 傳真／ (02) 2808-6545
郵政劃撥／ 31598840
戶名／哈福企業有限公司
出版日期／ 2022 年 10 月
定價／ NT$ 330 元 (附MP3)
港幣定價／ 110 元 (附MP3)
封面內文圖/ 取材自Shutterstock

全球華文國際市場總代理／采舍國際有限公司
地址／新北市中和區中山路2段366巷10號3樓
電話／(02) 8245-8786 傳真／(02) 8245-8718
網址／www.silkbook.com 新絲路華文網

香港澳門總經銷／和平圖書有限公司
地址／香港柴灣嘉業街12 號百樂門大廈17 樓
電話／ (852) 2804-6687
傳真／ (852) 2804-6409

email ／ welike8686@Gmail.com
facebook ／ Haa-net 哈福網路商城

電子書格式：PDF

國家圖書館出版品預行編目資料

輕鬆打開英語話匣子/蘇盈盈, Lily Thomas合
著. -- 新北市：哈福企業有限公司, 2022.10
　面；　公分. -- (英語系列；80)
ISBN 978-626-96215-7-6(平裝附光碟片)

1.CST: 英語 2.CST: 會話

805.188　　　　　　　　　　　　111015874